SHERLOCK HOLMES

and the Adventure of the Six Napoleons

Based on the stories of
Sir Arthur Conan Doyle

Adapted by **Murray Shaw** and **M. J. Cosson**
Illustrated by **Sophie Rohrbach** and **JT Morrow**

GRAPHIC UNIVERSE™ • MINNEAPOLIS • NEW YORK

Grateful acknowledgment to Dame Jean Conan Doyle for permission to use the Sherlock Holmes characters created by Sir Arthur Conan Doyle

Text copyright © 2012 by Murray Shaw
Illustrations © 2012 by Lerner Publishing Group, Inc.

Graphic Universe™ is a trademark of Lerner Publishing Group, Inc.

Graphic Universe™
A division of Lerner Publishing Group, Inc.
241 First Avenue North
Minneapolis, MN 55401 U.S.A.

Website address: www.lernerbooks.com

Library of Congress Cataloging-in-Publication Data

Shaw, Murray.
    Sherlock Holmes and the adventure of the six Napoleons / adapted by Murray Shaw and M.J. Cosson ; illustrated by Sophie Rohrbach and J.T. Morrow ; from the original stories by Sir Arthur Conan Doyle.
        p.   cm. — (On the case with Holmes and Watson ; #09)
    Summary: Retold in graphic novel form, Sherlock Holmes investigates why busts of Napoleon are being smashed throughout London. Includes a section explaining Holmes's reasoning and the clues he used to solve the mystery.
    ISBN: 978-0-7613-7088-8 (lib. bdg. : alk. paper)
    I. Graphic novels. (I. Graphic novels. 2. Doyle, Arthur Conan, Sir, 1859–1930. Adventure of the six Napoleons—Adaptations. 3. Mystery and detective stories. 4. London (England)—Fiction. 5. Great Britain—History—19th century—Fiction.) I. Cosson, M. J. II. Rohrbach, Sophie, ill. III. Morrow, J.T., ill. IV. Doyle, Arthur Conan, Sir, 1859–1930. Adventure of the six Napoleons. V. Title. VI. Title: Adventure of the six Napoleons.
PZ7.7.S46Shh 2011
741.5'973—dc22   2010031983

Manufactured in the United States of America
1—BC—7/15/11

The Story of
SHERLOCK HOLMES
the Famous Detective

Sherlock Holmes and his helpful friend Dr. John Watson are fictional characters created by British writer Sir Arthur Conan Doyle. Doyle published his first novel about the pair, *A Study in Scarlet*, in 1887, and it became very successful. Doyle went on to write fifty-six short stories, as well as three more novels about Holmes's adventures—*The Sign of Four* (1890), *The Hound of the Baskervilles* (1902), and *The Valley of Fear* (1915).

Sherlock Holmes and Dr. Watson have become some of the most famous book characters of all time. Holmes spent most of his time solving mysteries, but he also had a wide array of hobbies, such as playing the violin, boxing, and sword fighting. Watson, a retired army doctor, met Holmes through a mutual friend when Holmes was looking for a roommate. Watson lived with Holmes for several years at 221B Baker Street before marrying and moving out. However, after his marriage, Watson continued to assist Holmes with his cases.

The original versions of the Sherlock Holmes stories are still printed, and many have been made into movies and television shows. Readers continue to be impressed by Holmes's detective methods of observation and scientific reason.

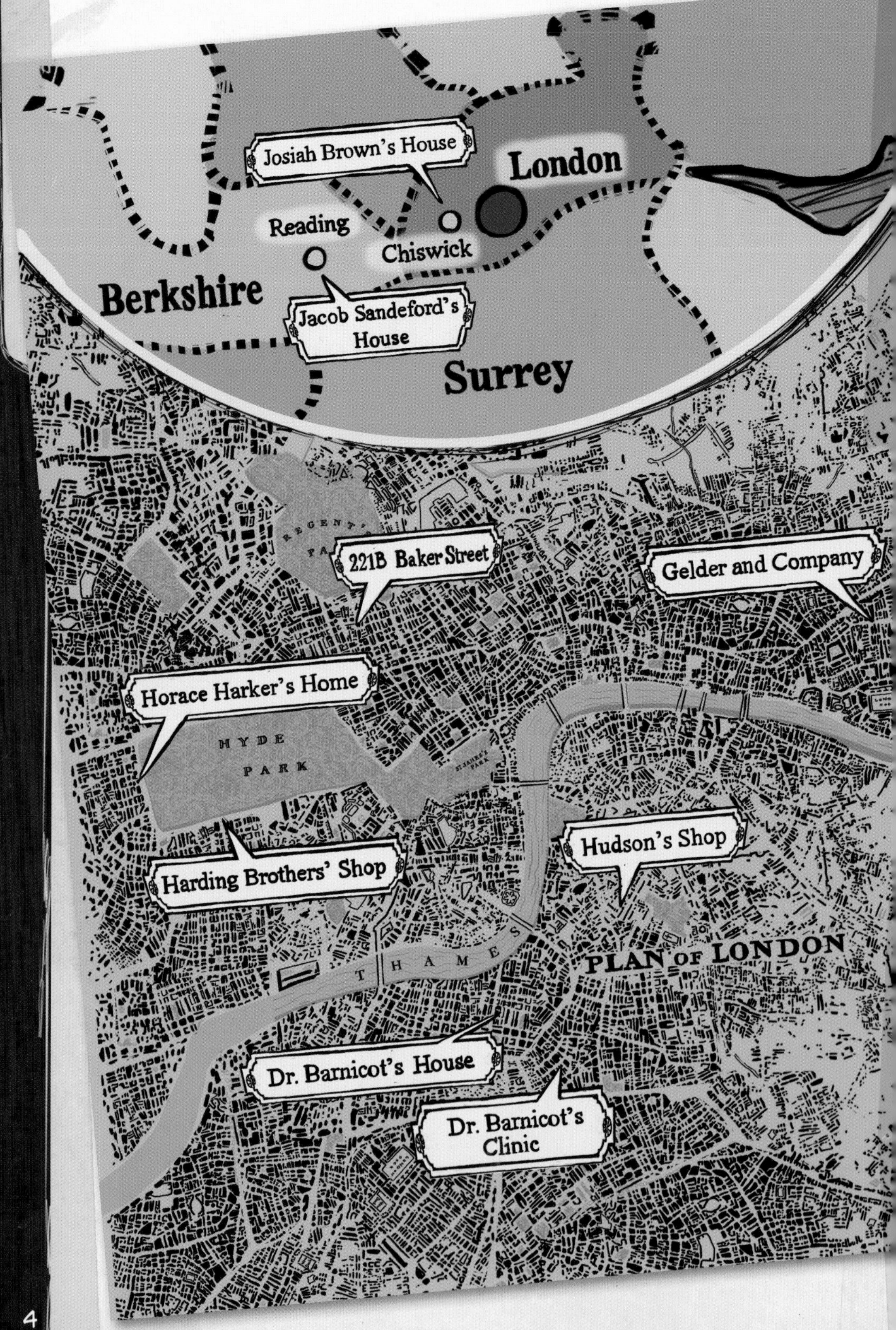
Josiah Brown's House
London
Reading
Chiswick
Berkshire
Jacob Sandeford's House
Surrey
REGENT'S PARK
221B Baker Street
Gelder and Company
Horace Harker's Home
HYDE PARK
ST. JAMES'S PARK
Hudson's Shop
Harding Brothers' Shop
THAMES
PLAN OF LONDON
Dr. Barnicot's House
Dr. Barnicot's Clinic

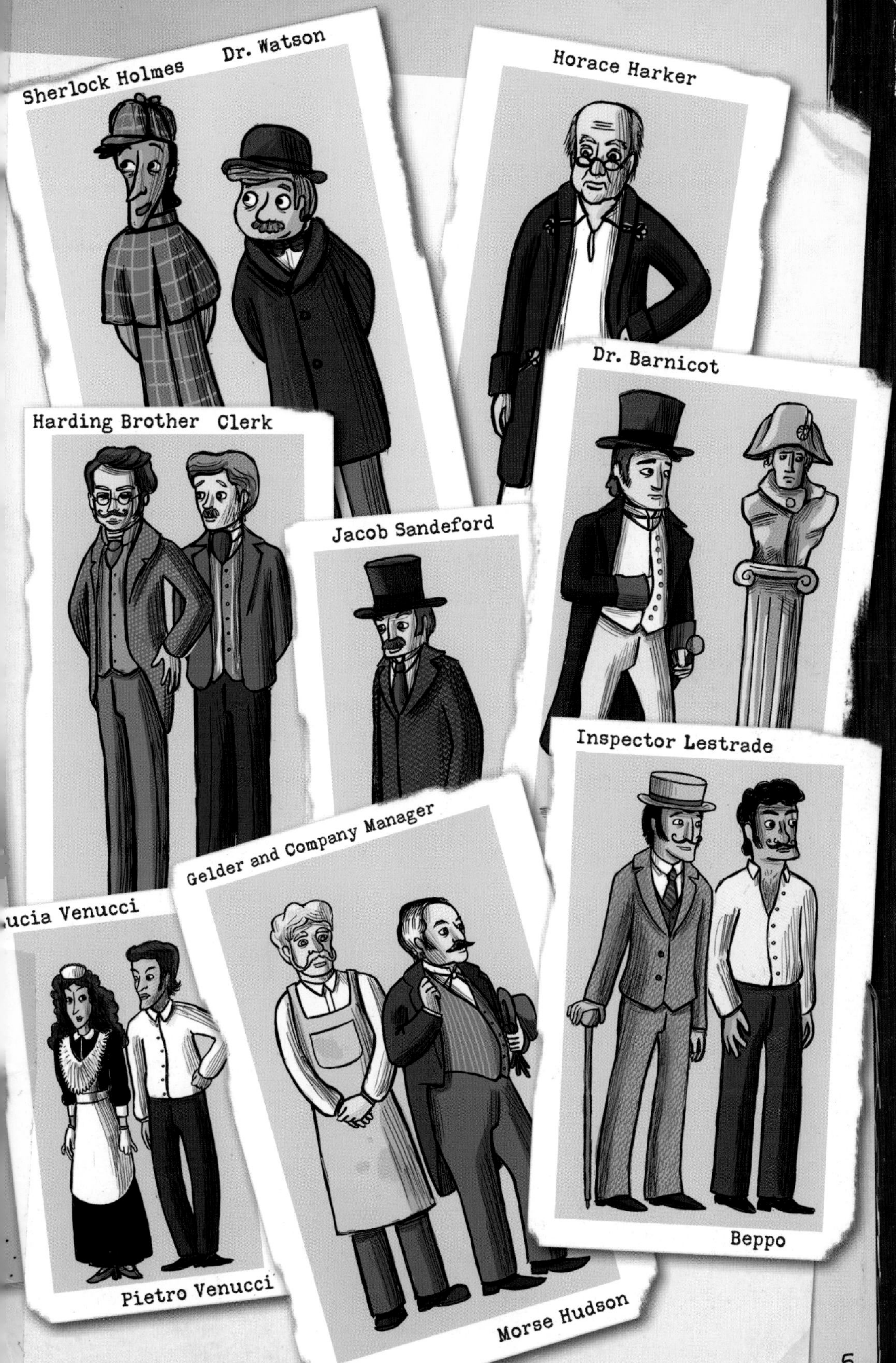
Sherlock Holmes
Dr. Watson
Horace Harker
Harding Brother
Clerk
Dr. Barnicot
Jacob Sandeford
Inspector Lestrade
Gelder and Company Manager
ucia Venucci
Pietro Venucci
Morse Hudson
Beppo

From the Desk of
John H. Watson, M.D.

My name is Dr. John H. Watson. For several years, I have been assisting my friend, Sherlock Holmes, in solving mysteries throughout the bustling city of London and beyond. Holmes is a peculiar man—always questioning and reasoning his way through various problems. But when I first met him in 1878, I was immediately intrigued by his oddities.

Holmes has always been more daring than I, and his logical deduction never ceases to amaze me. I have begun writing down all of the adventures I have with Holmes. This is one of those stories.

Sincerely,

Dr. Watson

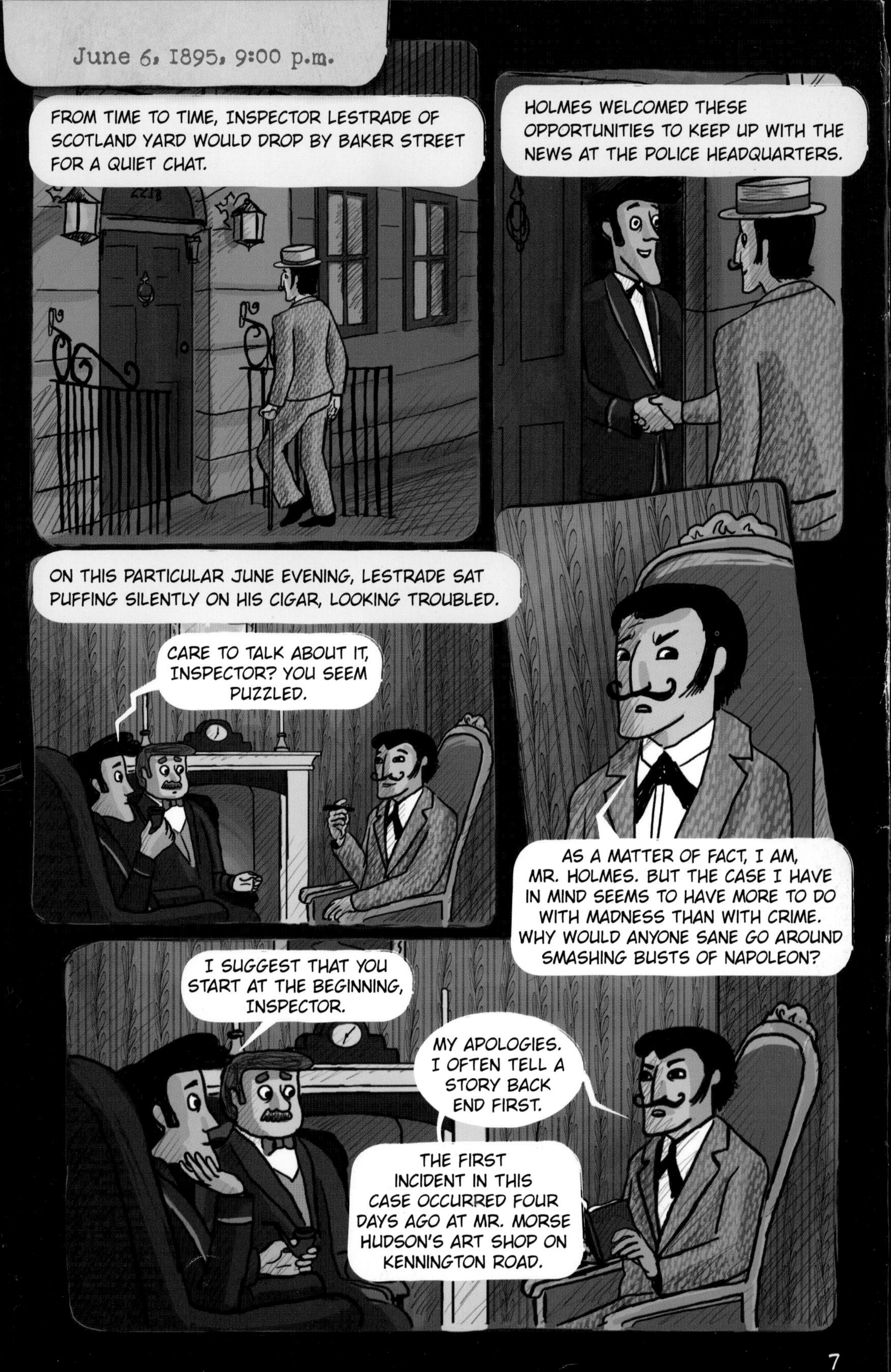

June 6, 1895, 9:00 p.m.
FROM TIME TO TIME, INSPECTOR LESTRADE OF SCOTLAND YARD WOULD DROP BY BAKER STREET FOR A QUIET CHAT.
HOLMES WELCOMED THESE OPPORTUNITIES TO KEEP UP WITH THE NEWS AT THE POLICE HEADQUARTERS.
ON THIS PARTICULAR JUNE EVENING, LESTRADE SAT PUFFING SILENTLY ON HIS CIGAR, LOOKING TROUBLED.
CARE TO TALK ABOUT IT, INSPECTOR? YOU SEEM PUZZLED.
AS A MATTER OF FACT, I AM, MR. HOLMES. BUT THE CASE I HAVE IN MIND SEEMS TO HAVE MORE TO DO WITH MADNESS THAN WITH CRIME. WHY WOULD ANYONE SANE GO AROUND SMASHING BUSTS OF NAPOLEON?
I SUGGEST THAT YOU START AT THE BEGINNING, INSPECTOR.
MY APOLOGIES. I OFTEN TELL A STORY BACK END FIRST.
THE FIRST INCIDENT IN THIS CASE OCCURRED FOUR DAYS AGO AT MR. MORSE HUDSON'S ART SHOP ON KENNINGTON ROAD.

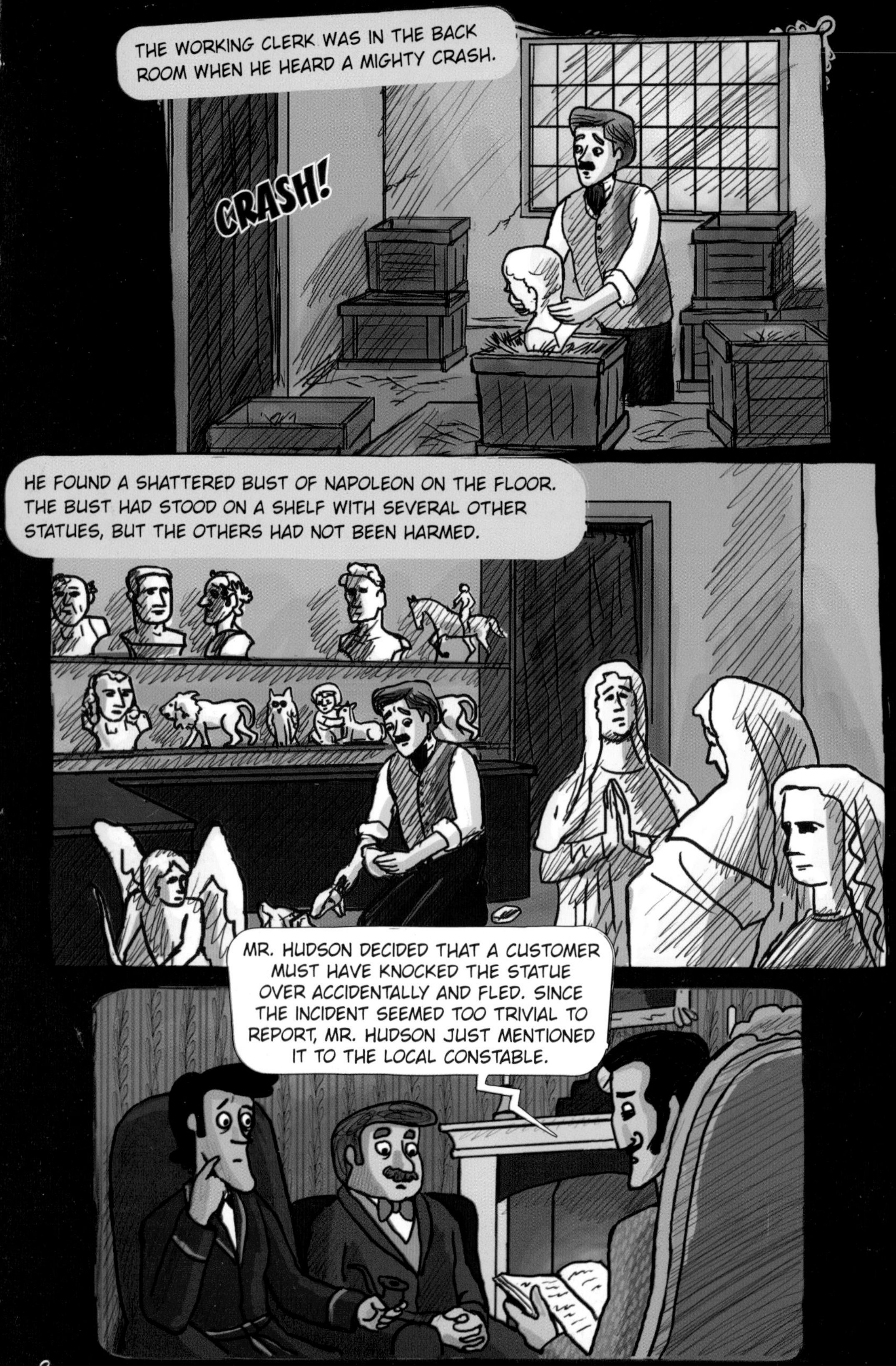
THE WORKING CLERK WAS IN THE BACK ROOM WHEN HE HEARD A MIGHTY CRASH.
CRASH!
HE FOUND A SHATTERED BUST OF NAPOLEON ON THE FLOOR. THE BUST HAD STOOD ON A SHELF WITH SEVERAL OTHER STATUES, BUT THE OTHERS HAD NOT BEEN HARMED.
MR. HUDSON DECIDED THAT A CUSTOMER MUST HAVE KNOCKED THE STATUE OVER ACCIDENTALLY AND FLED. SINCE THE INCIDENT SEEMED TOO TRIVIAL TO REPORT, MR. HUDSON JUST MENTIONED IT TO THE LOCAL CONSTABLE.

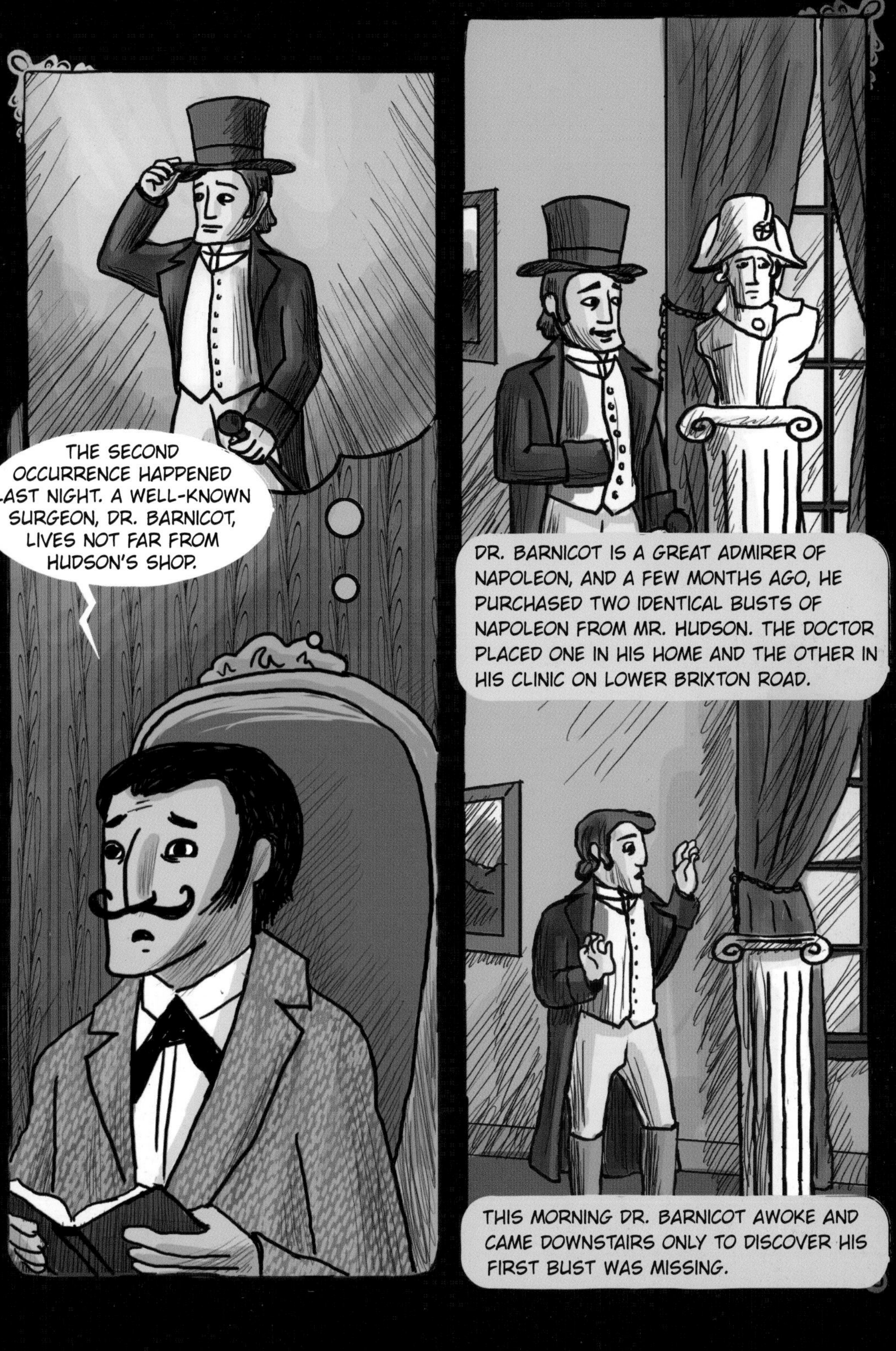
THE SECOND OCCURRENCE HAPPENED LAST NIGHT. A WELL-KNOWN SURGEON, DR. BARNICOT, LIVES NOT FAR FROM HUDSON'S SHOP.
DR. BARNICOT IS A GREAT ADMIRER OF NAPOLEON, AND A FEW MONTHS AGO, HE PURCHASED TWO IDENTICAL BUSTS OF NAPOLEON FROM MR. HUDSON. THE DOCTOR PLACED ONE IN HIS HOME AND THE OTHER IN HIS CLINIC ON LOWER BRIXTON ROAD.
THIS MORNING DR. BARNICOT AWOKE AND CAME DOWNSTAIRS ONLY TO DISCOVER HIS FIRST BUST WAS MISSING.

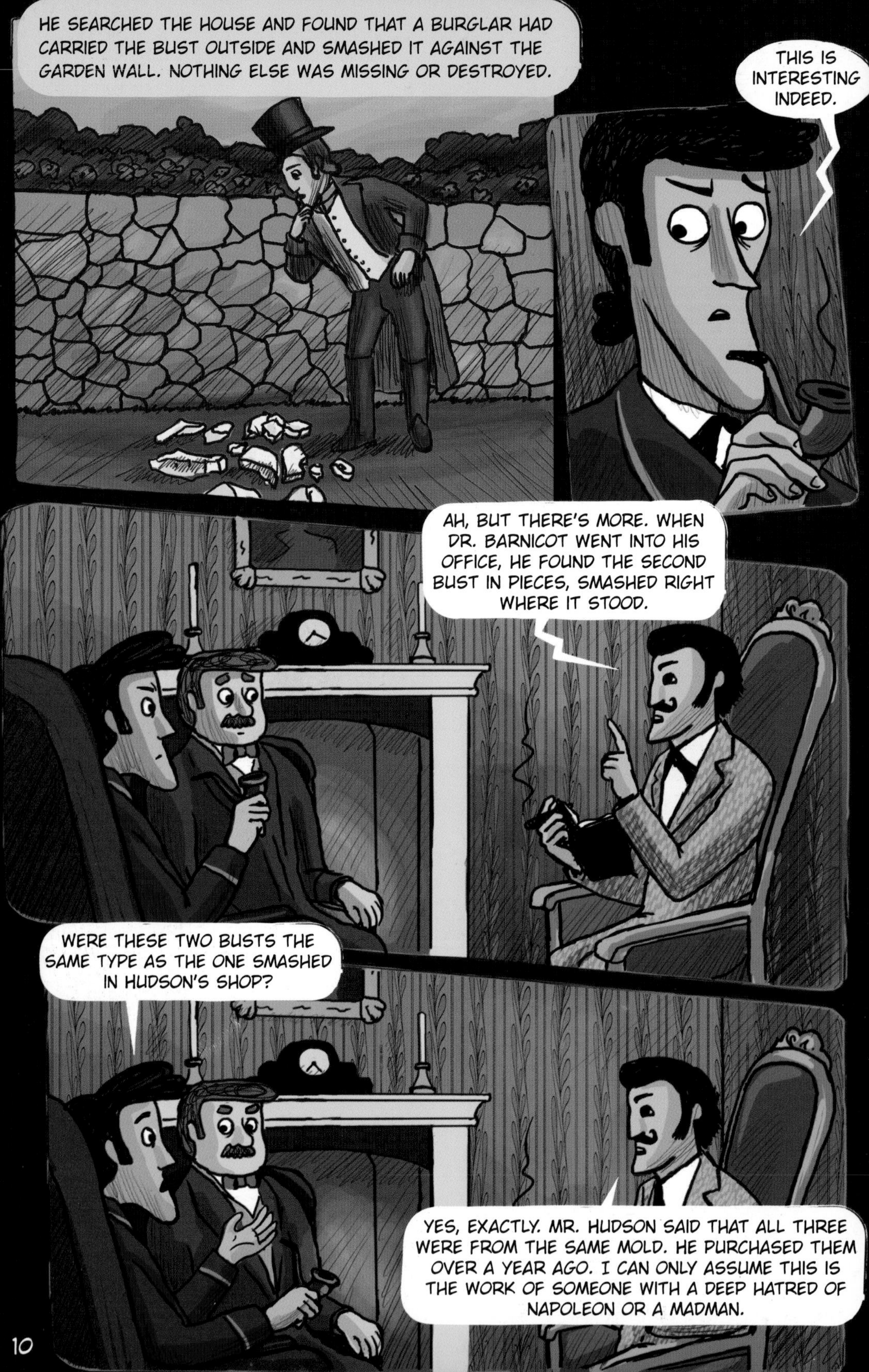
HE SEARCHED THE HOUSE AND FOUND THAT A BURGLAR HAD CARRIED THE BUST OUTSIDE AND SMASHED IT AGAINST THE GARDEN WALL. NOTHING ELSE WAS MISSING OR DESTROYED.
THIS IS INTERESTING INDEED.
AH, BUT THERE'S MORE. WHEN DR. BARNICOT WENT INTO HIS OFFICE, HE FOUND THE SECOND BUST IN PIECES, SMASHED RIGHT WHERE IT STOOD.
WERE THESE TWO BUSTS THE SAME TYPE AS THE ONE SMASHED IN HUDSON'S SHOP?
YES, EXACTLY. MR. HUDSON SAID THAT ALL THREE WERE FROM THE SAME MOLD. HE PURCHASED THEM OVER A YEAR AGO. I CAN ONLY ASSUME THIS IS THE WORK OF SOMEONE WITH A DEEP HATRED OF NAPOLEON OR A MADMAN.

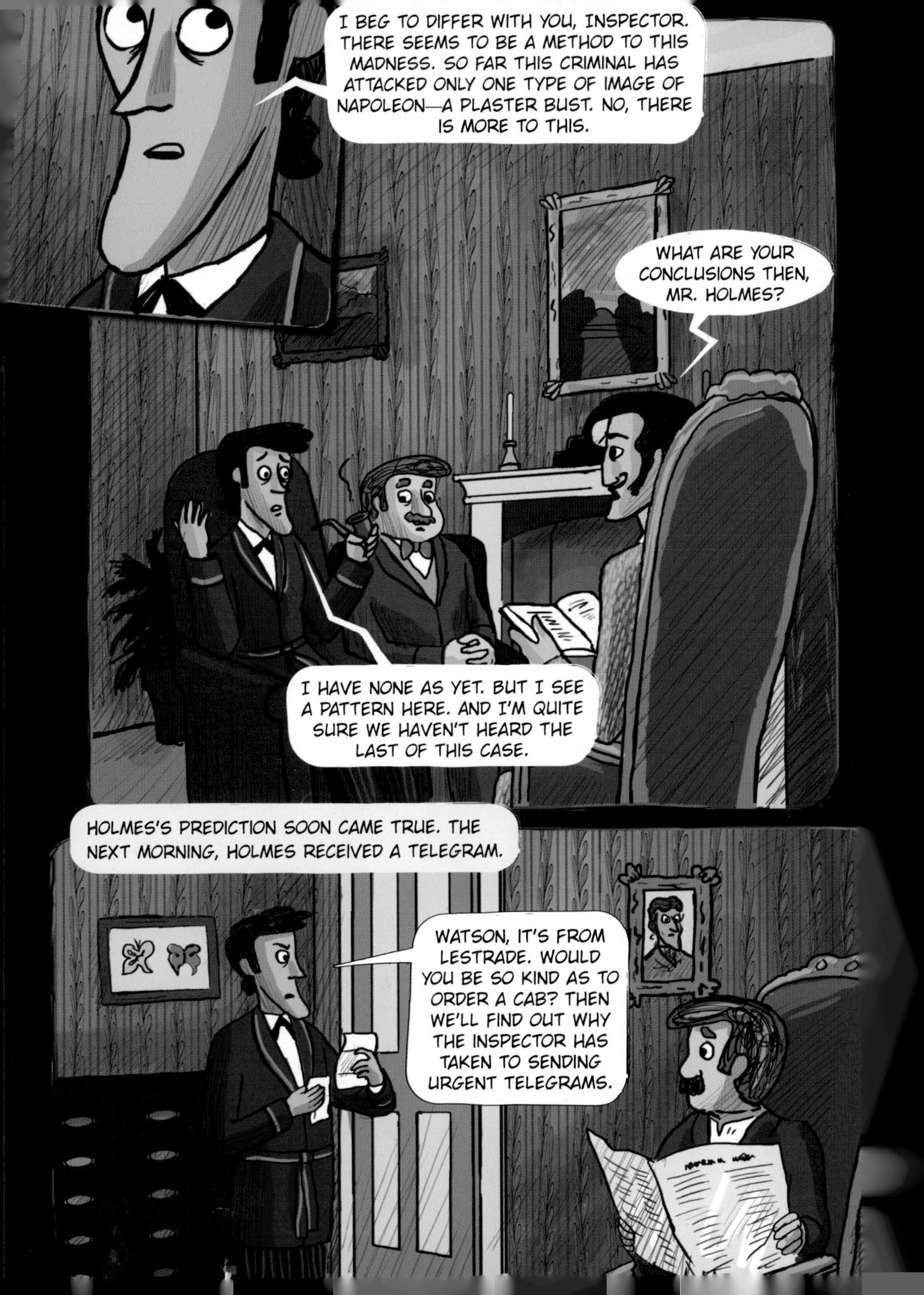
I BEG TO DIFFER WITH YOU, INSPECTOR. THERE SEEMS TO BE A METHOD TO THIS MADNESS. SO FAR THIS CRIMINAL HAS ATTACKED ONLY ONE TYPE OF IMAGE OF NAPOLEON—A PLASTER BUST. NO, THERE IS MORE TO THIS.
WHAT ARE YOUR CONCLUSIONS THEN, MR. HOLMES?
I HAVE NONE AS YET. BUT I SEE A PATTERN HERE. AND I'M QUITE SURE WE HAVEN'T HEARD THE LAST OF THIS CASE.
HOLMES'S PREDICTION SOON CAME TRUE. THE NEXT MORNING, HOLMES RECEIVED A TELEGRAM.
WATSON, IT'S FROM LESTRADE. WOULD YOU BE SO KIND AS TO ORDER A CAB? THEN WE'LL FIND OUT WHY THE INSPECTOR HAS TAKEN TO SENDING URGENT TELEGRAMS.

June 7, 1895, 8:00 a.m.

Within a quarter of an hour, our cab pulled up at Pitt Street, a land of plain row houses, dingy with dirt and soot. The police and a group of onlookers were standing around the middle house, number 131. Holmes whistled under his breath when he saw the activity surrounding the house.

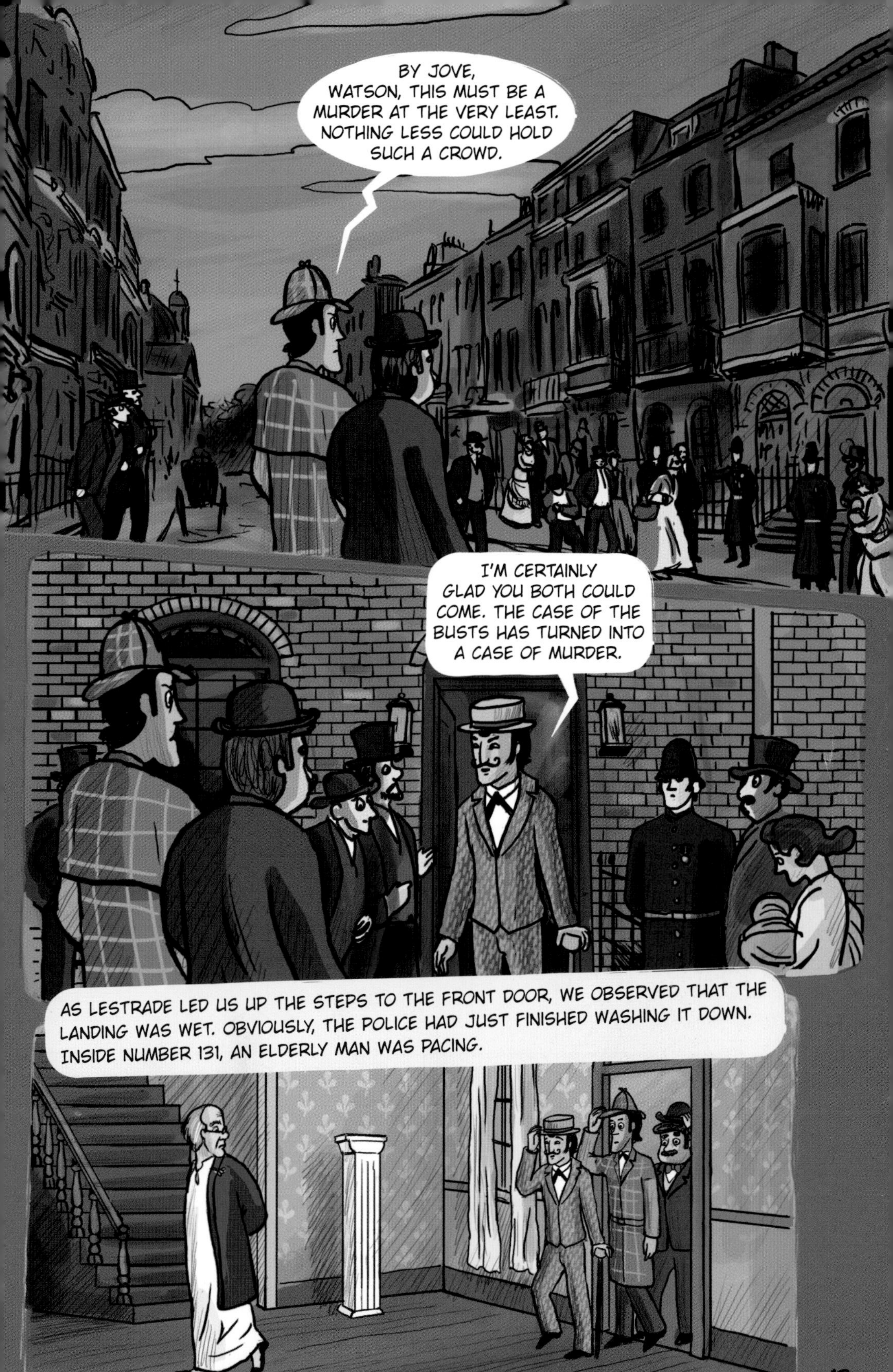
BY JOVE, WATSON, THIS MUST BE A MURDER AT THE VERY LEAST. NOTHING LESS COULD HOLD SUCH A CROWD.
I'M CERTAINLY GLAD YOU BOTH COULD COME. THE CASE OF THE BUSTS HAS TURNED INTO A CASE OF MURDER.
AS LESTRADE LED US UP THE STEPS TO THE FRONT DOOR, WE OBSERVED THAT THE LANDING WAS WET. OBVIOUSLY, THE POLICE HAD JUST FINISHED WASHING IT DOWN. INSIDE NUMBER 131, AN ELDERLY MAN WAS PACING.

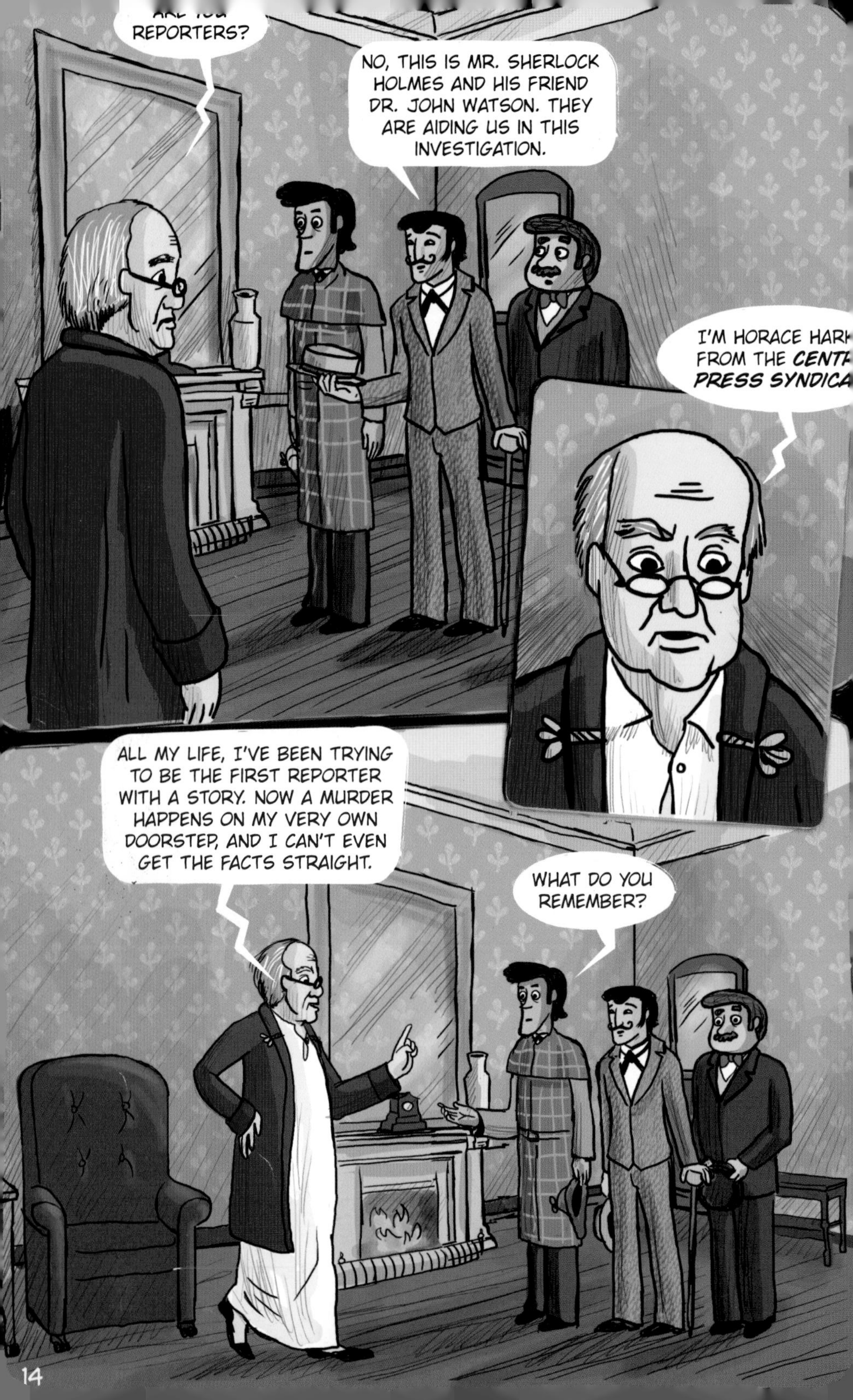

REPORTERS?
NO, THIS IS MR. SHERLOCK HOLMES AND HIS FRIEND DR. JOHN WATSON. THEY ARE AIDING US IN THIS INVESTIGATION.
I'M HORACE HARK FROM THE *CENTR* *PRESS SYNDICA*
ALL MY LIFE, I'VE BEEN TRYING TO BE THE FIRST REPORTER WITH A STORY. NOW A MURDER HAPPENS ON MY VERY OWN DOORSTEP, AND I CAN'T EVEN GET THE FACTS STRAIGHT.
WHAT DO YOU REMEMBER?

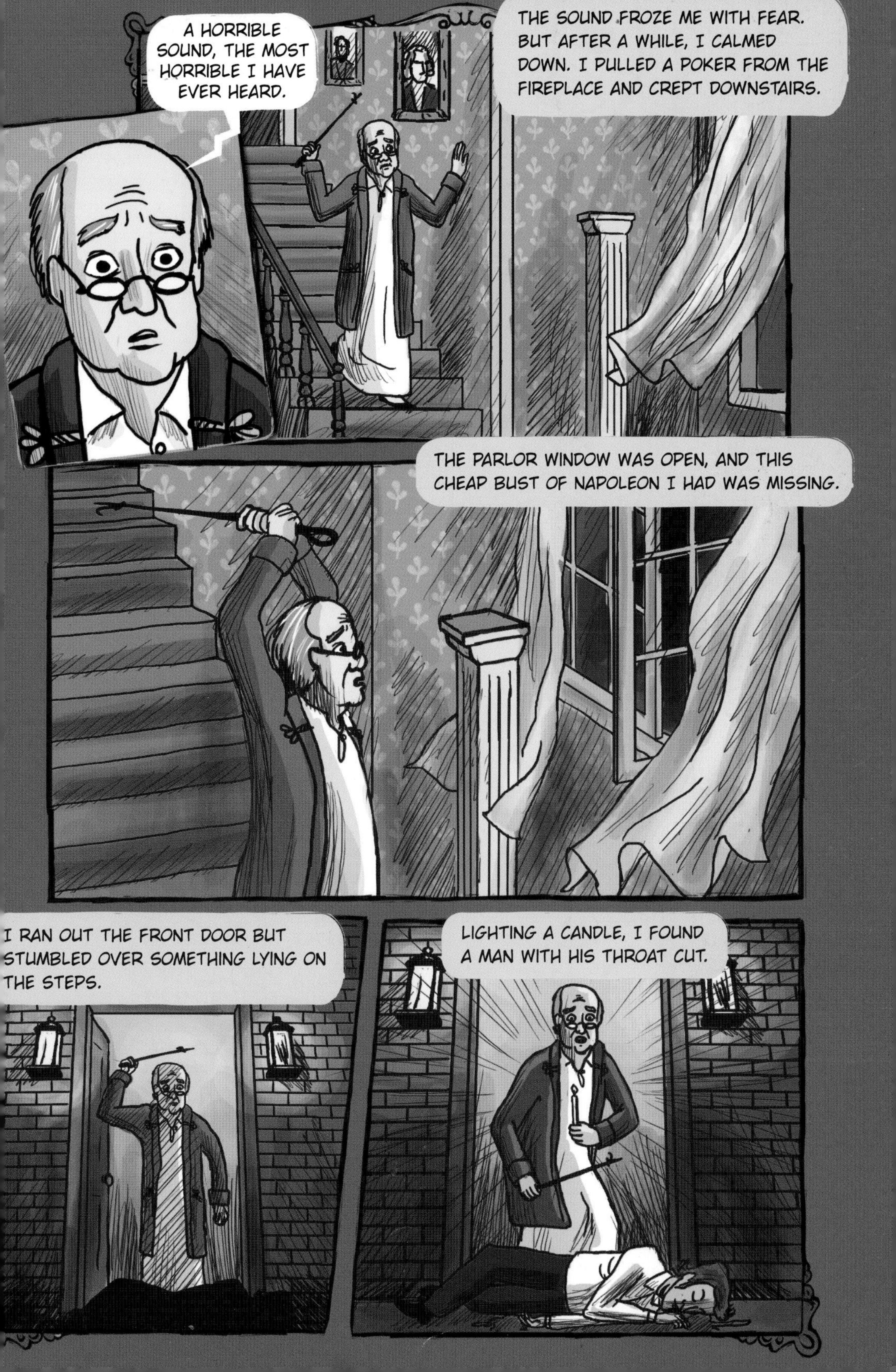
A HORRIBLE SOUND, THE MOST HORRIBLE I HAVE EVER HEARD.
THE SOUND FROZE ME WITH FEAR. BUT AFTER A WHILE, I CALMED DOWN. I PULLED A POKER FROM THE FIREPLACE AND CREPT DOWNSTAIRS.
THE PARLOR WINDOW WAS OPEN, AND THIS CHEAP BUST OF NAPOLEON I HAD WAS MISSING.
I RAN OUT THE FRONT DOOR BUT STUMBLED OVER SOMETHING LYING ON THE STEPS.
LIGHTING A CANDLE, I FOUND A MAN WITH HIS THROAT CUT.

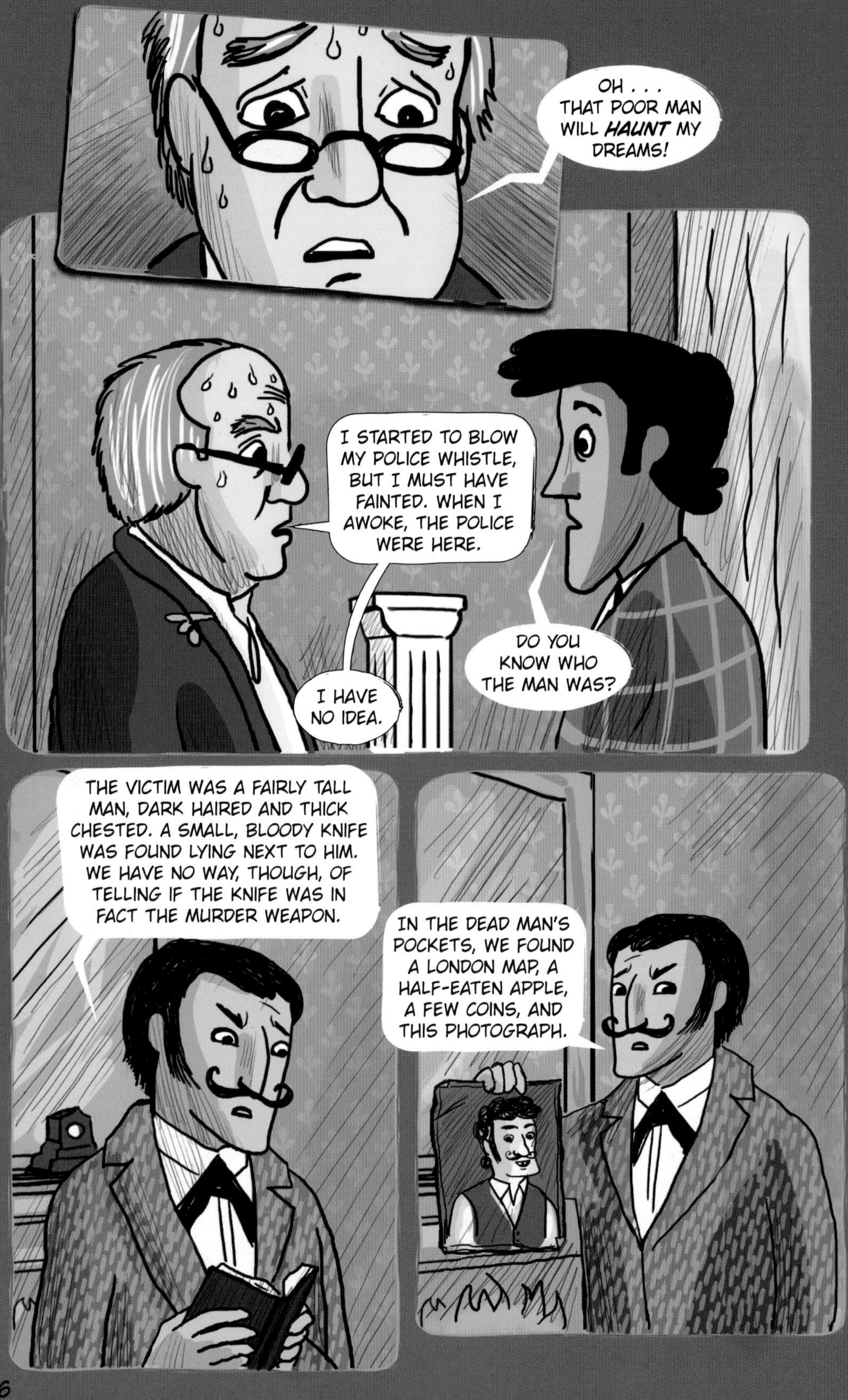
OH . . . THAT POOR MAN WILL HAUNT MY DREAMS!
I STARTED TO BLOW MY POLICE WHISTLE, BUT I MUST HAVE FAINTED. WHEN I AWOKE, THE POLICE WERE HERE.
DO YOU KNOW WHO THE MAN WAS?
I HAVE NO IDEA.
THE VICTIM WAS A FAIRLY TALL MAN, DARK HAIRED AND THICK CHESTED. A SMALL, BLOODY KNIFE WAS FOUND LYING NEXT TO HIM. WE HAVE NO WAY, THOUGH, OF TELLING IF THE KNIFE WAS IN FACT THE MURDER WEAPON.
IN THE DEAD MAN'S POCKETS, WE FOUND A LONDON MAP, A HALF-EATEN APPLE, A FEW COINS, AND THIS PHOTOGRAPH.

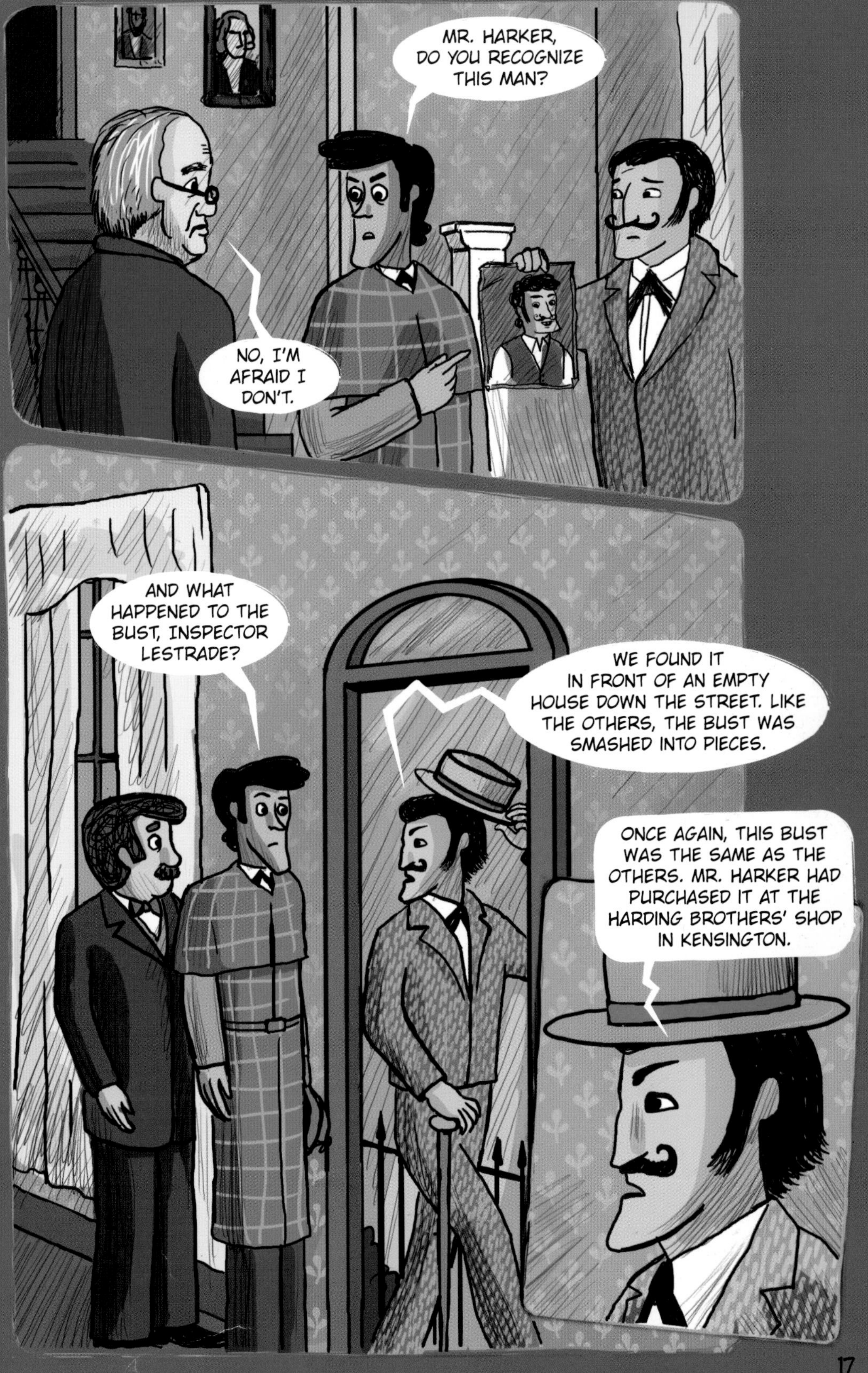
MR. HARKER, DO YOU RECOGNIZE THIS MAN?
NO, I'M AFRAID I DON'T.
AND WHAT HAPPENED TO THE BUST, INSPECTOR LESTRADE?
WE FOUND IT IN FRONT OF AN EMPTY HOUSE DOWN THE STREET. LIKE THE OTHERS, THE BUST WAS SMASHED INTO PIECES.
ONCE AGAIN, THIS BUST WAS THE SAME AS THE OTHERS. MR. HARKER HAD PURCHASED IT AT THE HARDING BROTHERS' SHOP IN KENSINGTON.

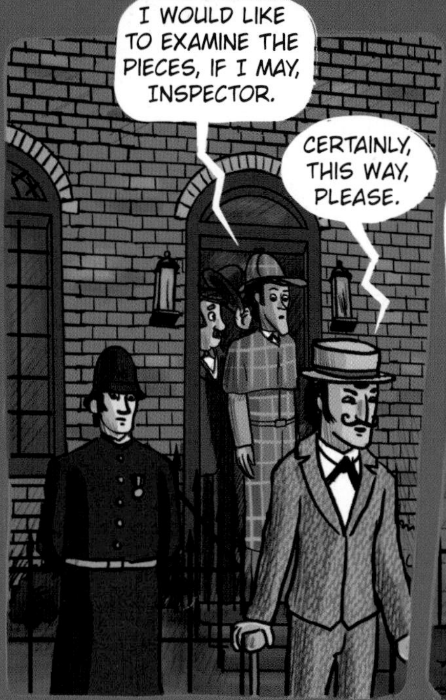
I WOULD LIKE TO EXAMINE THE PIECES, IF I MAY, INSPECTOR.
CERTAINLY, THIS WAY, PLEASE.

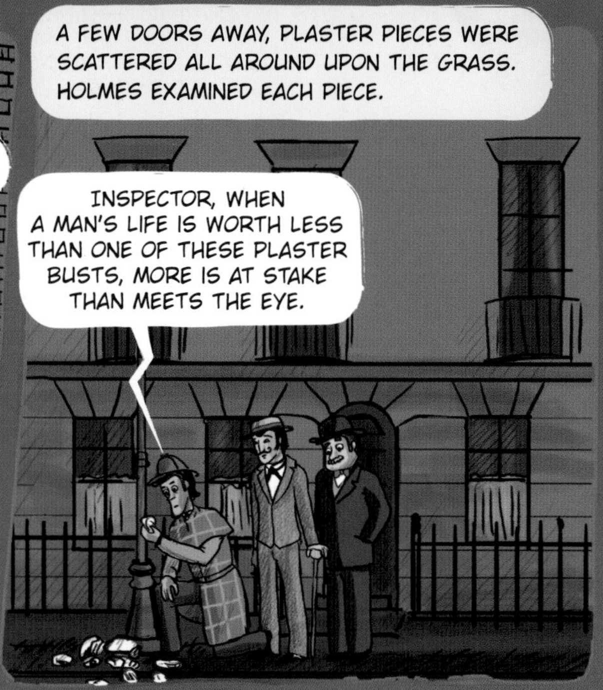
A FEW DOORS AWAY, PLASTER PIECES WERE SCATTERED ALL AROUND UPON THE GRASS. HOLMES EXAMINED EACH PIECE.
INSPECTOR, WHEN A MAN'S LIFE IS WORTH LESS THAN ONE OF THESE PLASTER BUSTS, MORE IS AT STAKE THAN MEETS THE EYE.

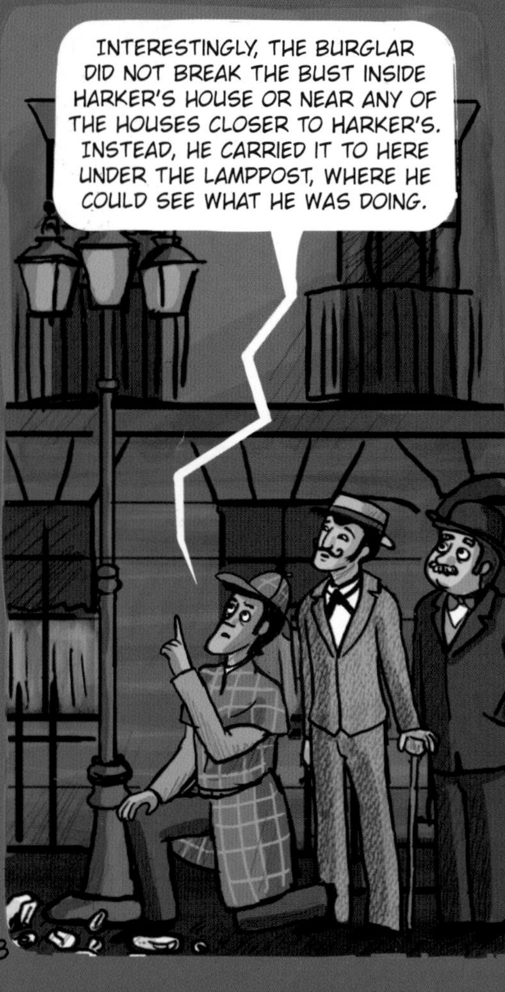
INTERESTINGLY, THE BURGLAR DID NOT BREAK THE BUST INSIDE HARKER'S HOUSE OR NEAR ANY OF THE HOUSES CLOSER TO HARKER'S. INSTEAD, HE CARRIED IT TO HERE UNDER THE LAMPPOST, WHERE HE COULD SEE WHAT HE WAS DOING.

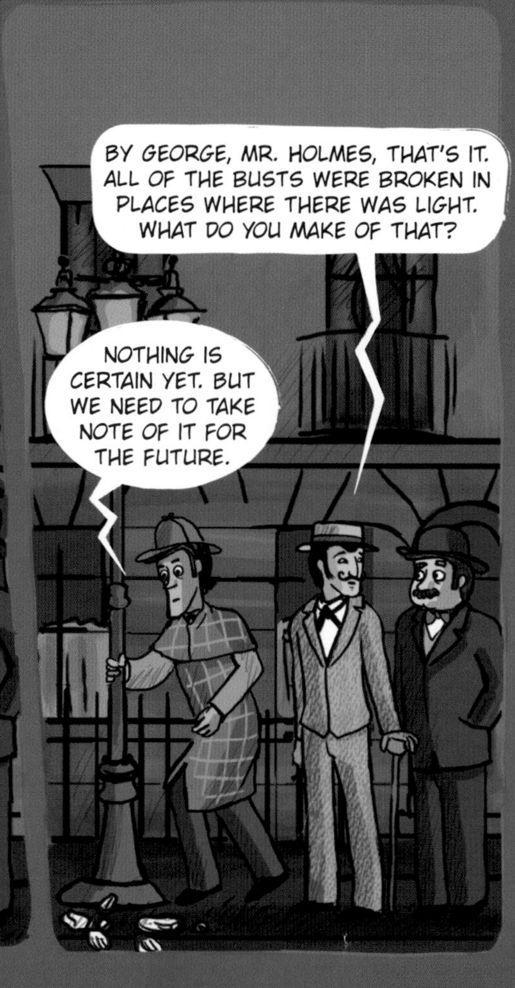
BY GEORGE, MR. HOLMES, THAT'S IT. ALL OF THE BUSTS WERE BROKEN IN PLACES WHERE THERE WAS LIGHT. WHAT DO YOU MAKE OF THAT?
NOTHING IS CERTAIN YET. BUT WE NEED TO TAKE NOTE OF IT FOR THE FUTURE.

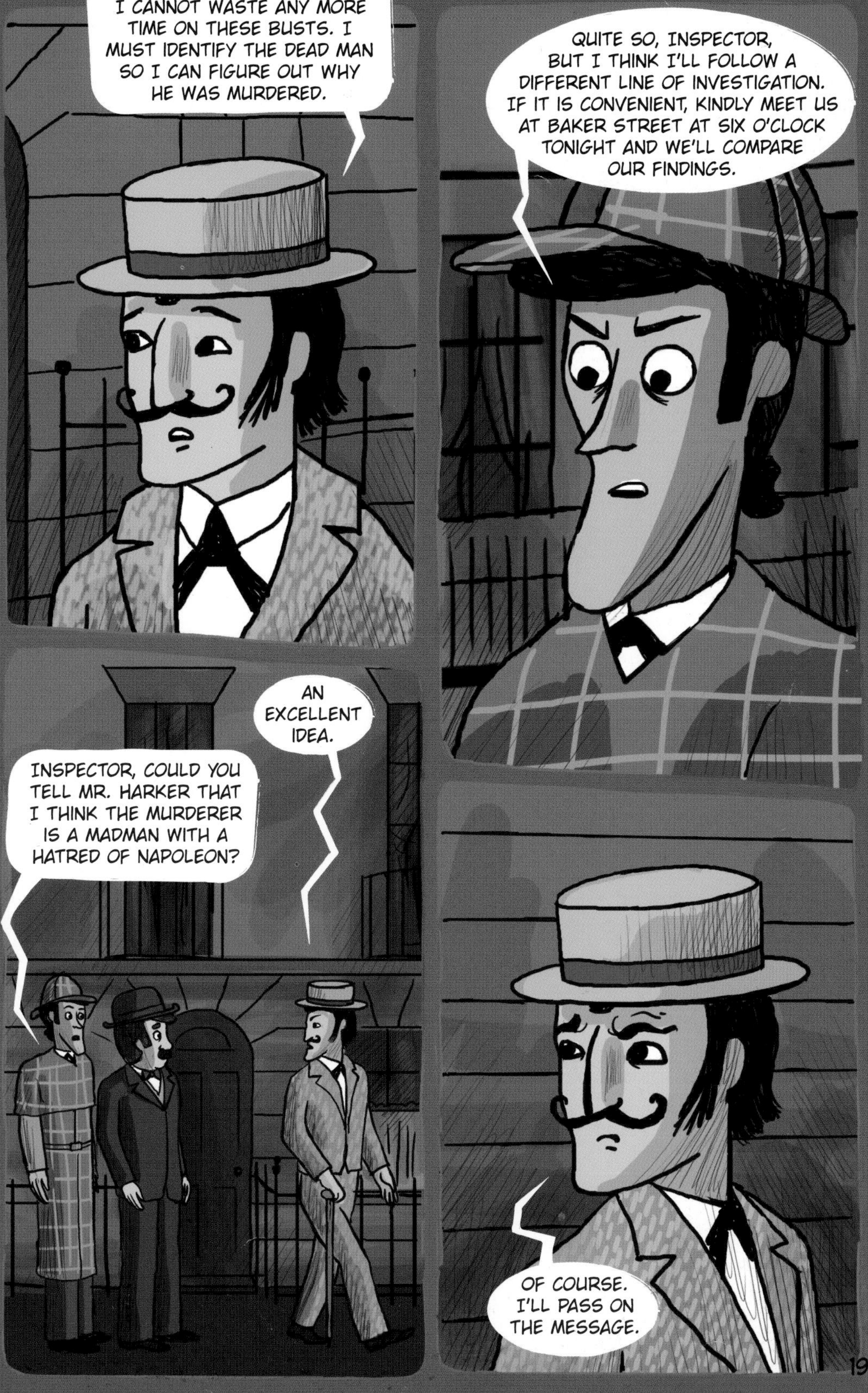
UNFORTUNATELY, MR. HOLMES, I CANNOT WASTE ANY MORE TIME ON THESE BUSTS. I MUST IDENTIFY THE DEAD MAN SO I CAN FIGURE OUT WHY HE WAS MURDERED.
QUITE SO, INSPECTOR, BUT I THINK I'LL FOLLOW A DIFFERENT LINE OF INVESTIGATION. IF IT IS CONVENIENT, KINDLY MEET US AT BAKER STREET AT SIX O'CLOCK TONIGHT AND WE'LL COMPARE OUR FINDINGS.
AN EXCELLENT IDEA.
INSPECTOR, COULD YOU TELL MR. HARKER THAT I THINK THE MURDERER IS A MADMAN WITH A HATRED OF NAPOLEON?
OF COURSE. I'LL PASS ON THE MESSAGE.

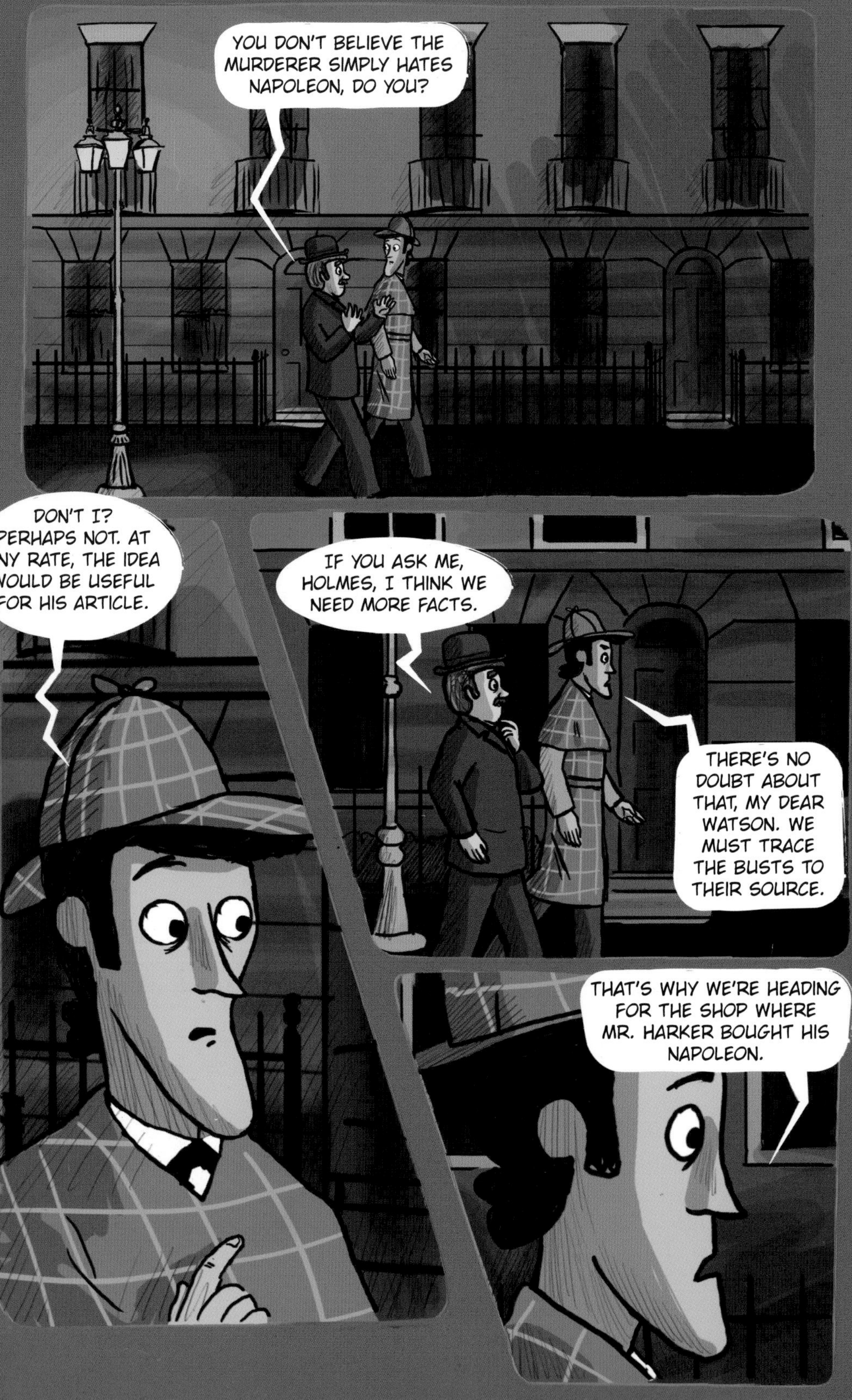
YOU DON'T BELIEVE THE MURDERER SIMPLY HATES NAPOLEON, DO YOU?
DON'T I? PERHAPS NOT. AT ANY RATE, THE IDEA WOULD BE USEFUL FOR HIS ARTICLE.
IF YOU ASK ME, HOLMES, I THINK WE NEED MORE FACTS.
THERE'S NO DOUBT ABOUT THAT, MY DEAR WATSON. WE MUST TRACE THE BUSTS TO THEIR SOURCE.
THAT'S WHY WE'RE HEADING FOR THE SHOP WHERE MR. HARKER BOUGHT HIS NAPOLEON.

Unfortunately, when we reached Harding Brothers' shop, the clerk told us that he was new to the job. He had no information for us. He advised us to return in the afternoon when one of the brothers would be in. We were frustrated, but we knew we couldn't expect the investigation to be easy. Holmes suggested that we make our way to Hudson's shop on Kennington Road instead.

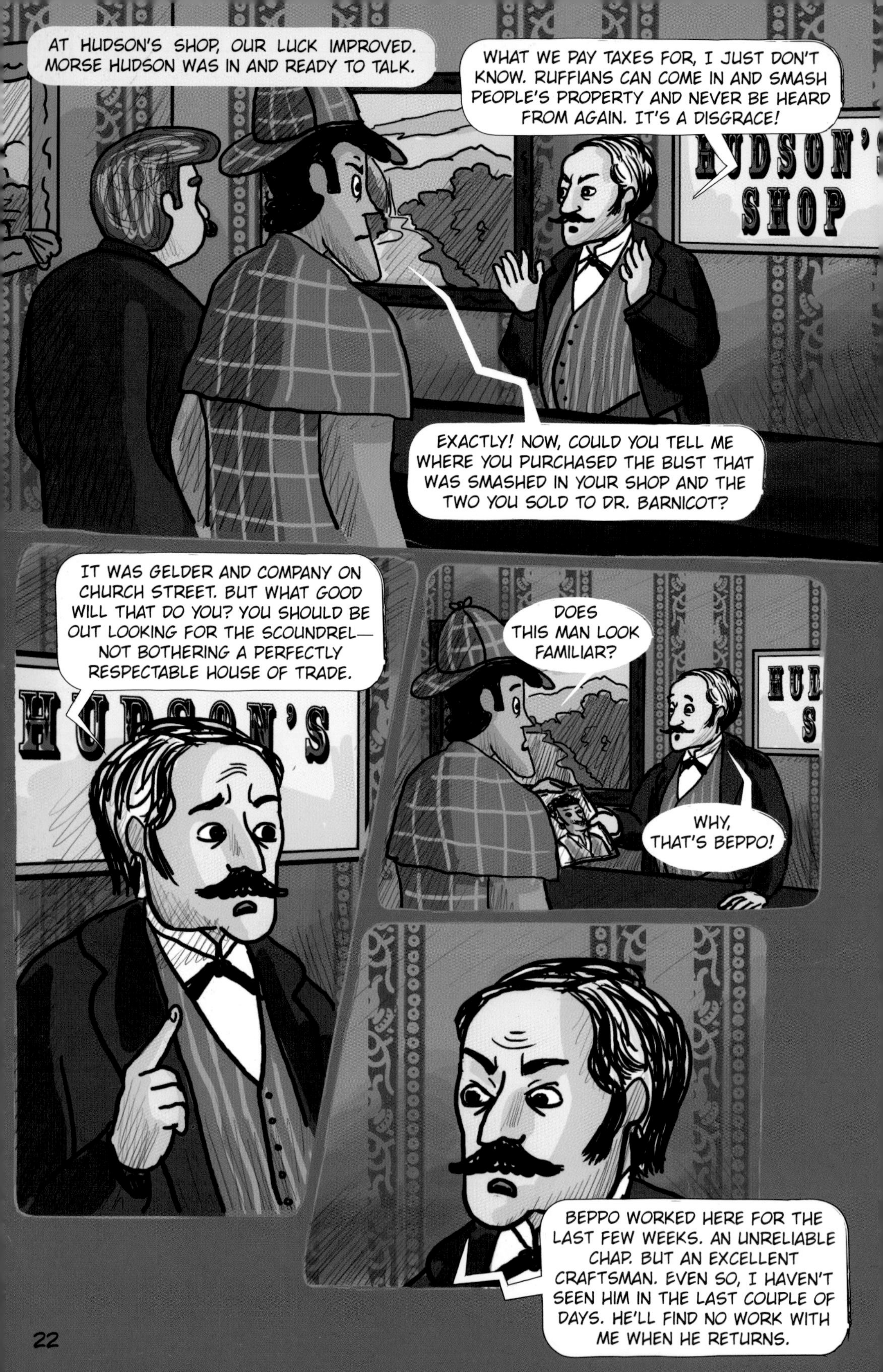
AT HUDSON'S SHOP, OUR LUCK IMPROVED. MORSE HUDSON WAS IN AND READY TO TALK.
WHAT WE PAY TAXES FOR, I JUST DON'T KNOW. RUFFIANS CAN COME IN AND SMASH PEOPLE'S PROPERTY AND NEVER BE HEARD FROM AGAIN. IT'S A DISGRACE!
HUDSON'S SHOP
EXACTLY! NOW, COULD YOU TELL ME WHERE YOU PURCHASED THE BUST THAT WAS SMASHED IN YOUR SHOP AND THE TWO YOU SOLD TO DR. BARNICOT?
IT WAS GELDER AND COMPANY ON CHURCH STREET. BUT WHAT GOOD WILL THAT DO YOU? YOU SHOULD BE OUT LOOKING FOR THE SCOUNDREL— NOT BOTHERING A PERFECTLY RESPECTABLE HOUSE OF TRADE.
DOES THIS MAN LOOK FAMILIAR?
WHY, THAT'S BEPPO!
BEPPO WORKED HERE FOR THE LAST FEW WEEKS. AN UNRELIABLE CHAP. BUT AN EXCELLENT CRAFTSMAN. EVEN SO, I HAVEN'T SEEN HIM IN THE LAST COUPLE OF DAYS. HE'LL FIND NO WORK WITH ME WHEN HE RETURNS.

Holmes thanked Hudson, and we left. We hailed a cab for south London and traveled along the Thames River to the dock district. Here we found Gelder and Company. Enormous statues filled the yard outside the warehouse. Inside the building, fifty or so workmen were carving stone or molding plaster. As we entered, a large, blond man introduced himself as the manager. Holmes began plying him with questions.

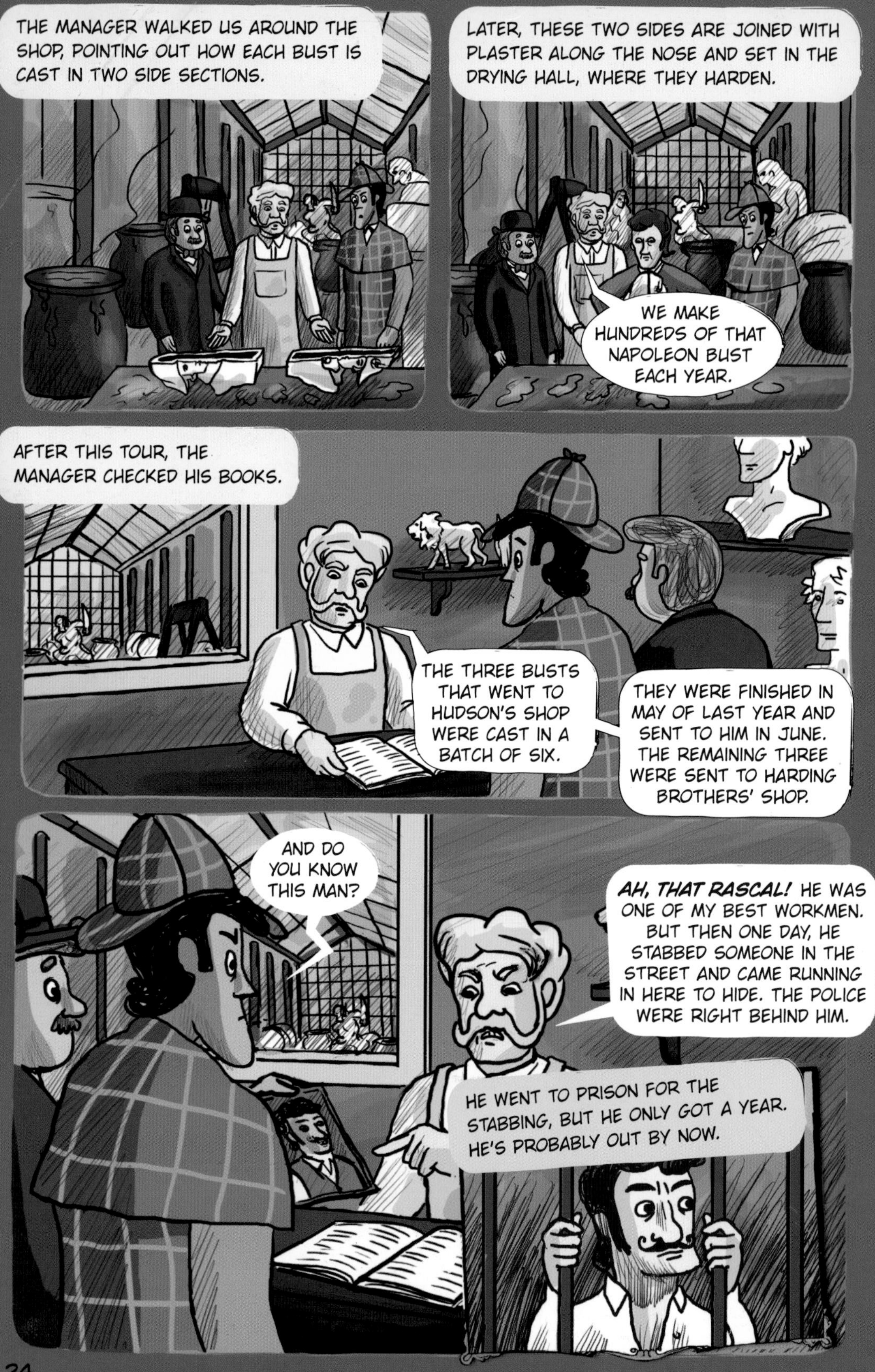
THE MANAGER WALKED US AROUND THE SHOP, POINTING OUT HOW EACH BUST IS CAST IN TWO SIDE SECTIONS.
LATER, THESE TWO SIDES ARE JOINED WITH PLASTER ALONG THE NOSE AND SET IN THE DRYING HALL, WHERE THEY HARDEN.
WE MAKE HUNDREDS OF THAT NAPOLEON BUST EACH YEAR.
AFTER THIS TOUR, THE MANAGER CHECKED HIS BOOKS.
THE THREE BUSTS THAT WENT TO HUDSON'S SHOP WERE CAST IN A BATCH OF SIX.
THEY WERE FINISHED IN MAY OF LAST YEAR AND SENT TO HIM IN JUNE. THE REMAINING THREE WERE SENT TO HARDING BROTHERS' SHOP.
AND DO YOU KNOW THIS MAN?
AH, THAT RASCAL! HE WAS ONE OF MY BEST WORKMEN. BUT THEN ONE DAY, HE STABBED SOMEONE IN THE STREET AND CAME RUNNING IN HERE TO HIDE. THE POLICE WERE RIGHT BEHIND HIM.
HE WENT TO PRISON FOR THE STABBING, BUT HE ONLY GOT A YEAR. HE'S PROBABLY OUT BY NOW.

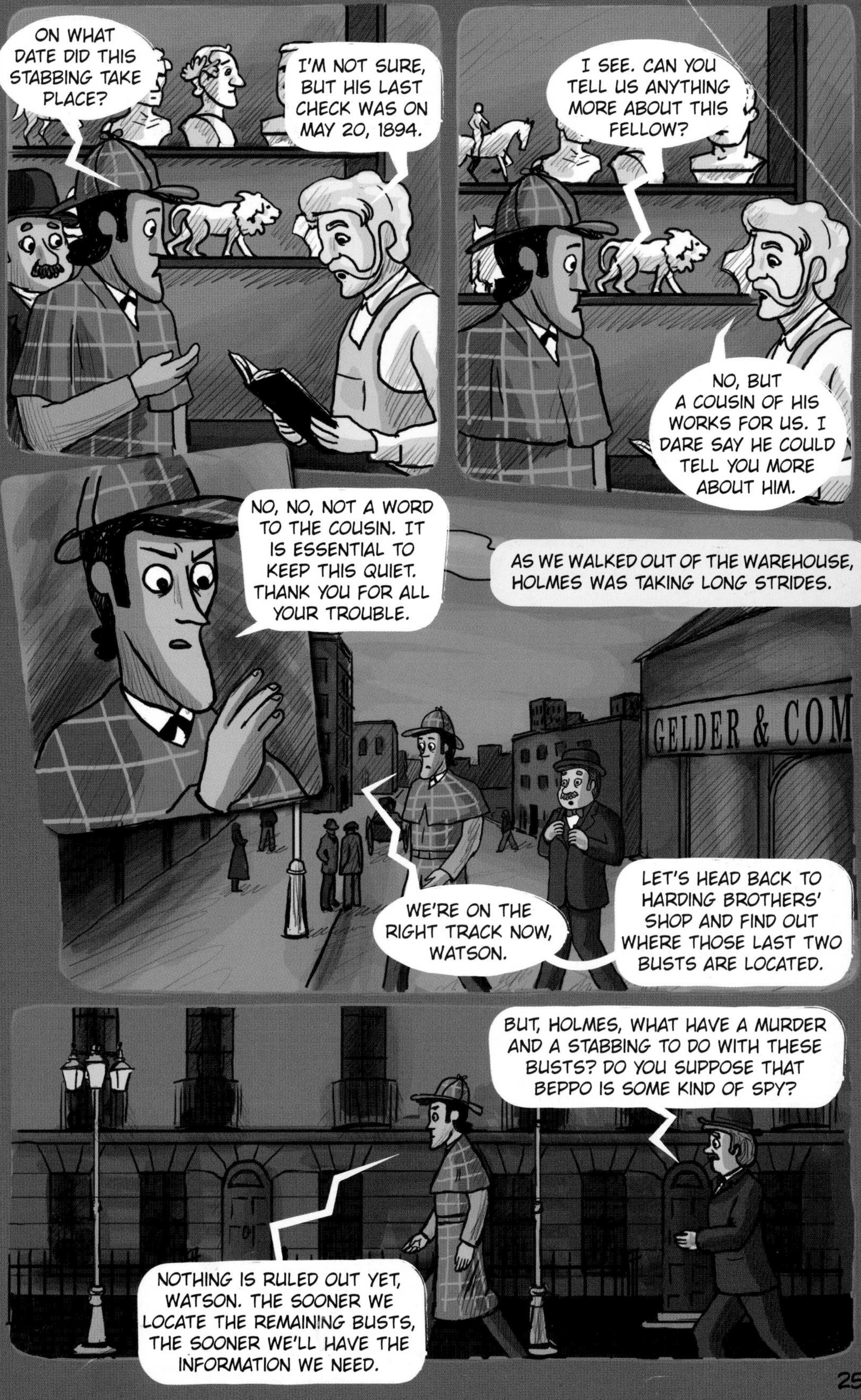
ON WHAT DATE DID THIS STABBING TAKE PLACE?
I'M NOT SURE, BUT HIS LAST CHECK WAS ON MAY 20, 1894.
I SEE. CAN YOU TELL US ANYTHING MORE ABOUT THIS FELLOW?
NO, BUT A COUSIN OF HIS WORKS FOR US. I DARE SAY HE COULD TELL YOU MORE ABOUT HIM.
NO, NO, NOT A WORD TO THE COUSIN. IT IS ESSENTIAL TO KEEP THIS QUIET. THANK YOU FOR ALL YOUR TROUBLE.
AS WE WALKED OUT OF THE WAREHOUSE, HOLMES WAS TAKING LONG STRIDES.
GELDER & COM
WE'RE ON THE RIGHT TRACK NOW, WATSON.
LET'S HEAD BACK TO HARDING BROTHERS' SHOP AND FIND OUT WHERE THOSE LAST TWO BUSTS ARE LOCATED.
BUT, HOLMES, WHAT HAVE A MURDER AND A STABBING TO DO WITH THESE BUSTS? DO YOU SUPPOSE THAT BEPPO IS SOME KIND OF SPY?
NOTHING IS RULED OUT YET, WATSON. THE SOONER WE LOCATE THE REMAINING BUSTS, THE SOONER WE'LL HAVE THE INFORMATION WE NEED.

On the way to Harding Brothers' shop, we took in a quick lunch at a small pub. Our attention was attracted by the headlines at a newsstand: "KENSINGTON SLASHING. MADMAN MURDERS OUT OF HATE FOR NAPOLEON." Holmes and I chuckled. Horace Harker had finally written the big story he wanted, and it was sweeping London. Once the murderer read it, the killer would never suspect that Holmes was hot on the trail.

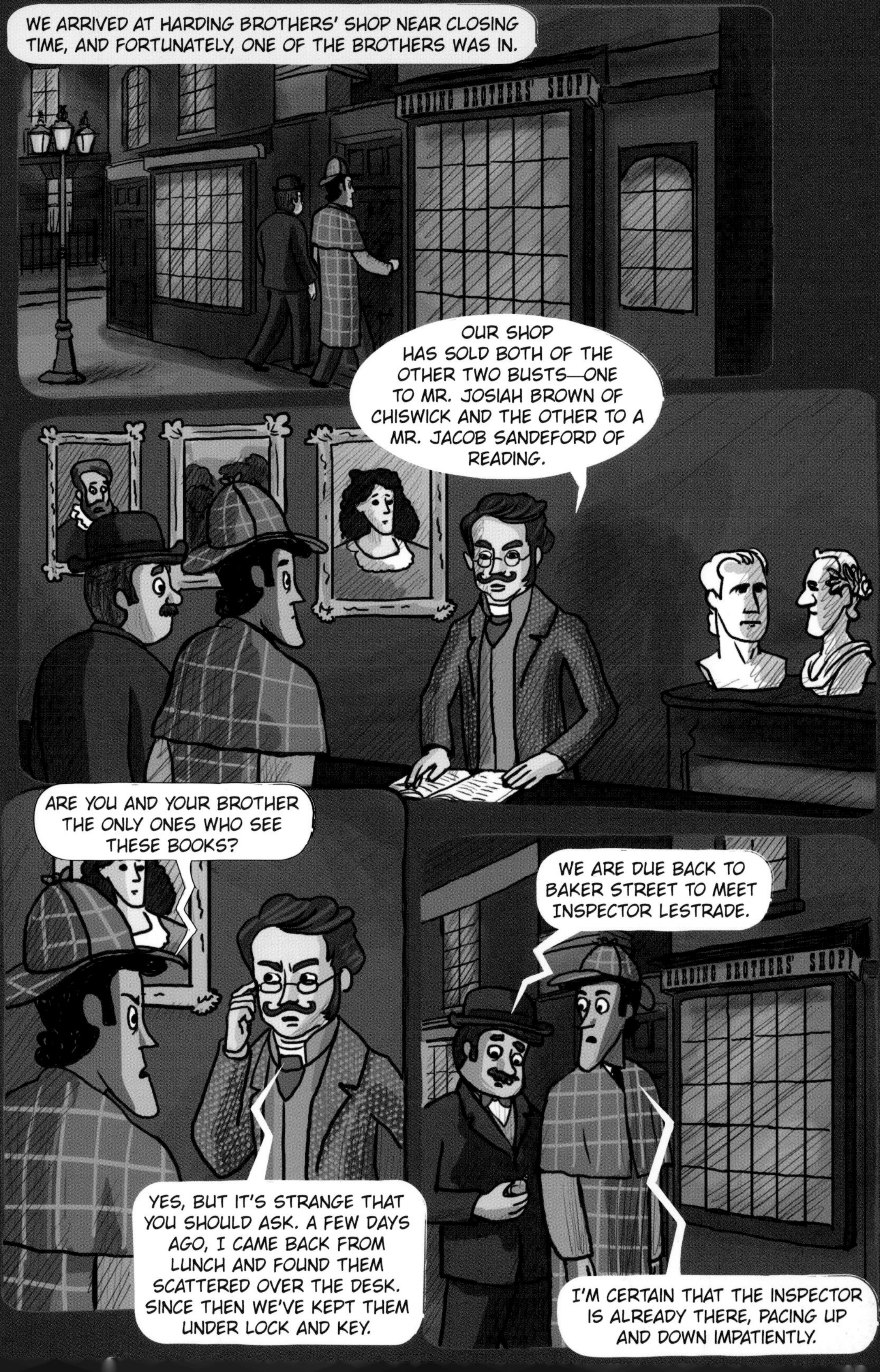
WE ARRIVED AT HARDING BROTHERS' SHOP NEAR CLOSING TIME, AND FORTUNATELY, ONE OF THE BROTHERS WAS IN.
HARDING BROTHERS' SHOP
OUR SHOP HAS SOLD BOTH OF THE OTHER TWO BUSTS—ONE TO MR. JOSIAH BROWN OF CHISWICK AND THE OTHER TO A MR. JACOB SANDEFORD OF READING.
ARE YOU AND YOUR BROTHER THE ONLY ONES WHO SEE THESE BOOKS?
YES, BUT IT'S STRANGE THAT YOU SHOULD ASK. A FEW DAYS AGO, I CAME BACK FROM LUNCH AND FOUND THEM SCATTERED OVER THE DESK. SINCE THEN WE'VE KEPT THEM UNDER LOCK AND KEY.
WE ARE DUE BACK TO BAKER STREET TO MEET INSPECTOR LESTRADE.
HARDING BROTHERS' SHOP
I'M CERTAIN THAT THE INSPECTOR IS ALREADY THERE, PACING UP AND DOWN IMPATIENTLY.

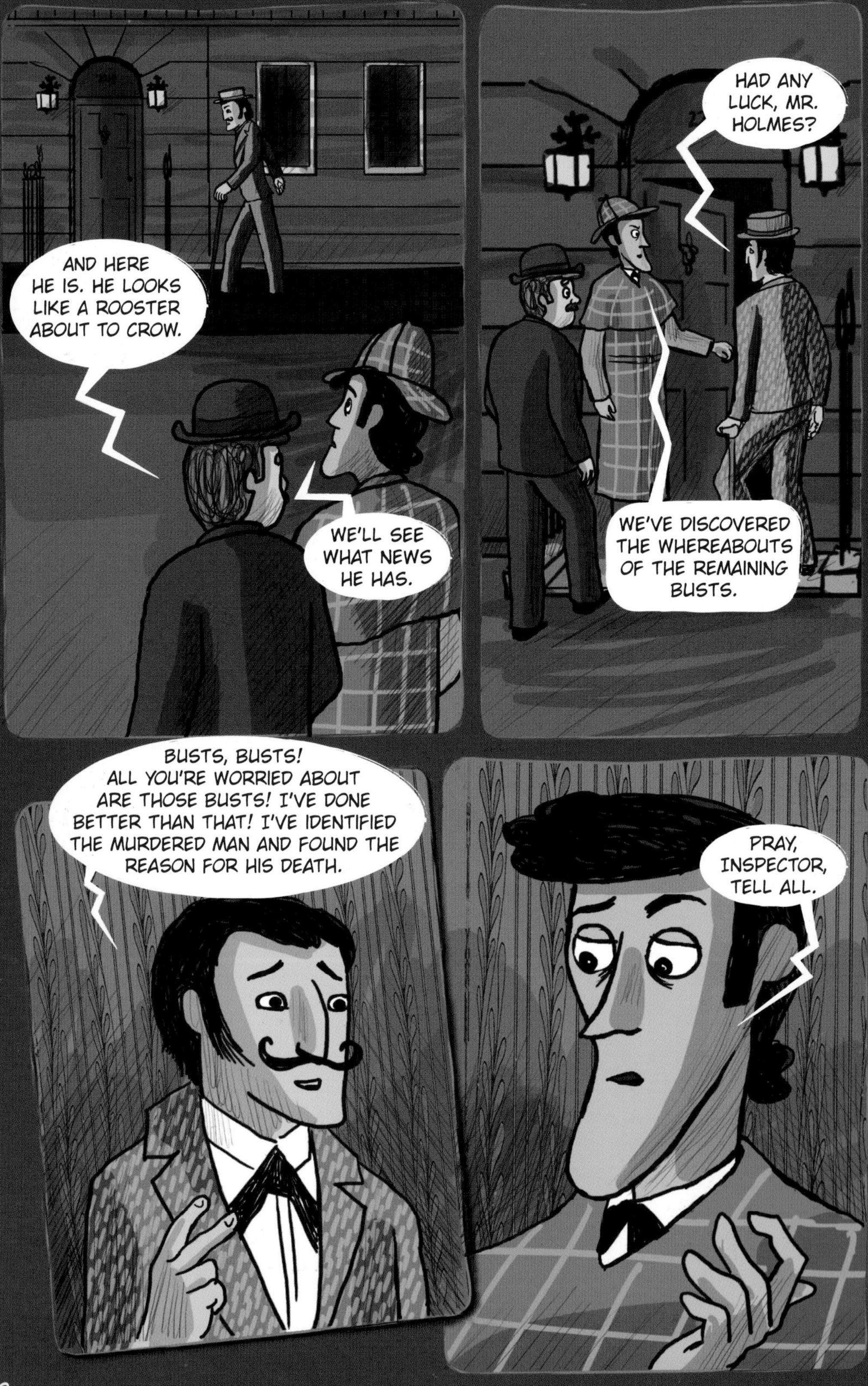
AND HERE HE IS. HE LOOKS LIKE A ROOSTER ABOUT TO CROW.
WE'LL SEE WHAT NEWS HE HAS.
HAD ANY LUCK, MR. HOLMES?
WE'VE DISCOVERED THE WHEREABOUTS OF THE REMAINING BUSTS.
BUSTS, BUSTS! ALL YOU'RE WORRIED ABOUT ARE THOSE BUSTS! I'VE DONE BETTER THAN THAT! I'VE IDENTIFIED THE MURDERED MAN AND FOUND THE REASON FOR HIS DEATH.
PRAY, INSPECTOR, TELL ALL.

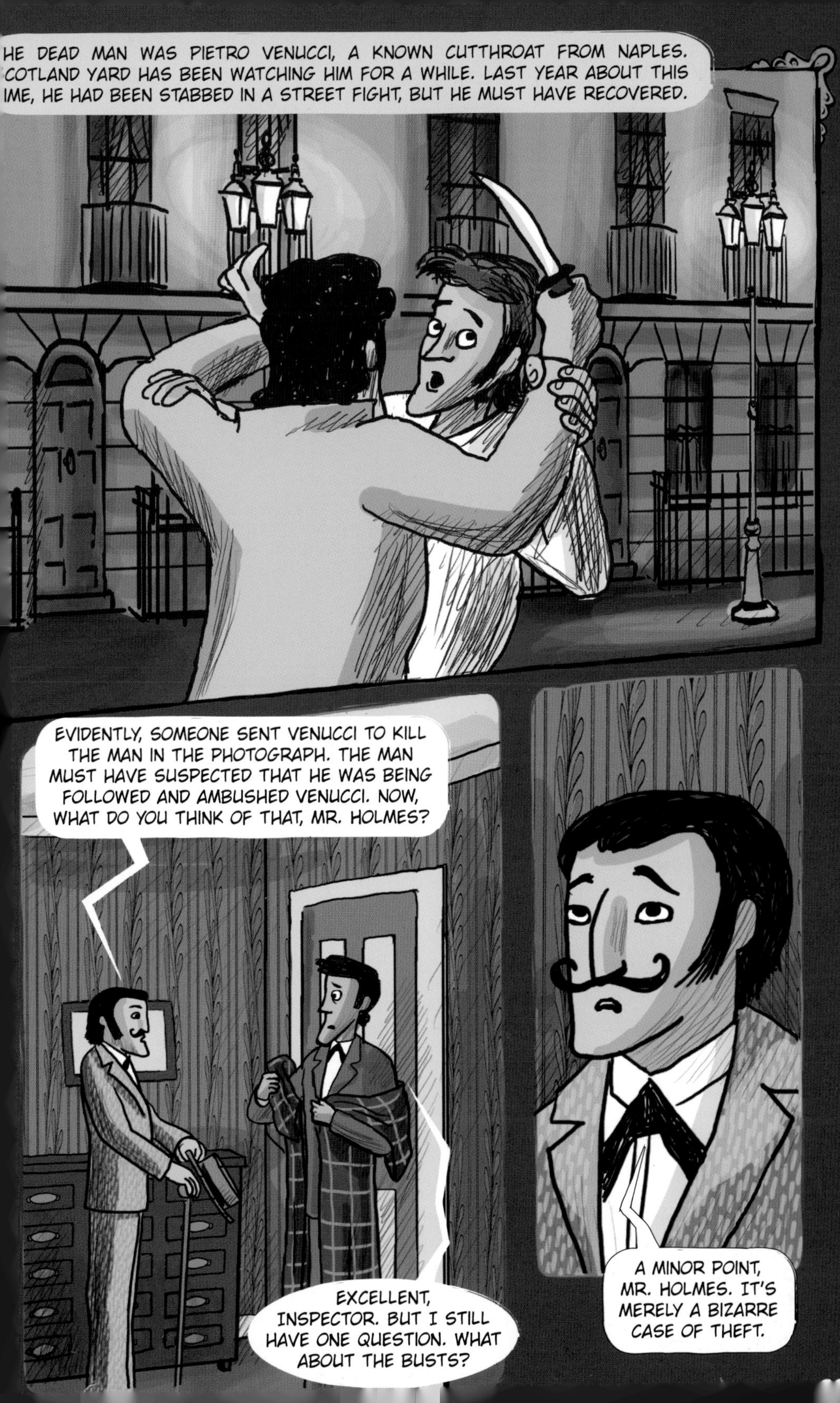
HE DEAD MAN WAS PIETRO VENUCCI, A KNOWN CUTTHROAT FROM NAPLES. COTLAND YARD HAS BEEN WATCHING HIM FOR A WHILE. LAST YEAR ABOUT THIS IME, HE HAD BEEN STABBED IN A STREET FIGHT, BUT HE MUST HAVE RECOVERED.
EVIDENTLY, SOMEONE SENT VENUCCI TO KILL THE MAN IN THE PHOTOGRAPH. THE MAN MUST HAVE SUSPECTED THAT HE WAS BEING FOLLOWED AND AMBUSHED VENUCCI. NOW, WHAT DO YOU THINK OF THAT, MR. HOLMES?
EXCELLENT, INSPECTOR. BUT I STILL HAVE ONE QUESTION. WHAT ABOUT THE BUSTS?
A MINOR POINT, MR. HOLMES. IT'S MERELY A BIZARRE CASE OF THEFT.

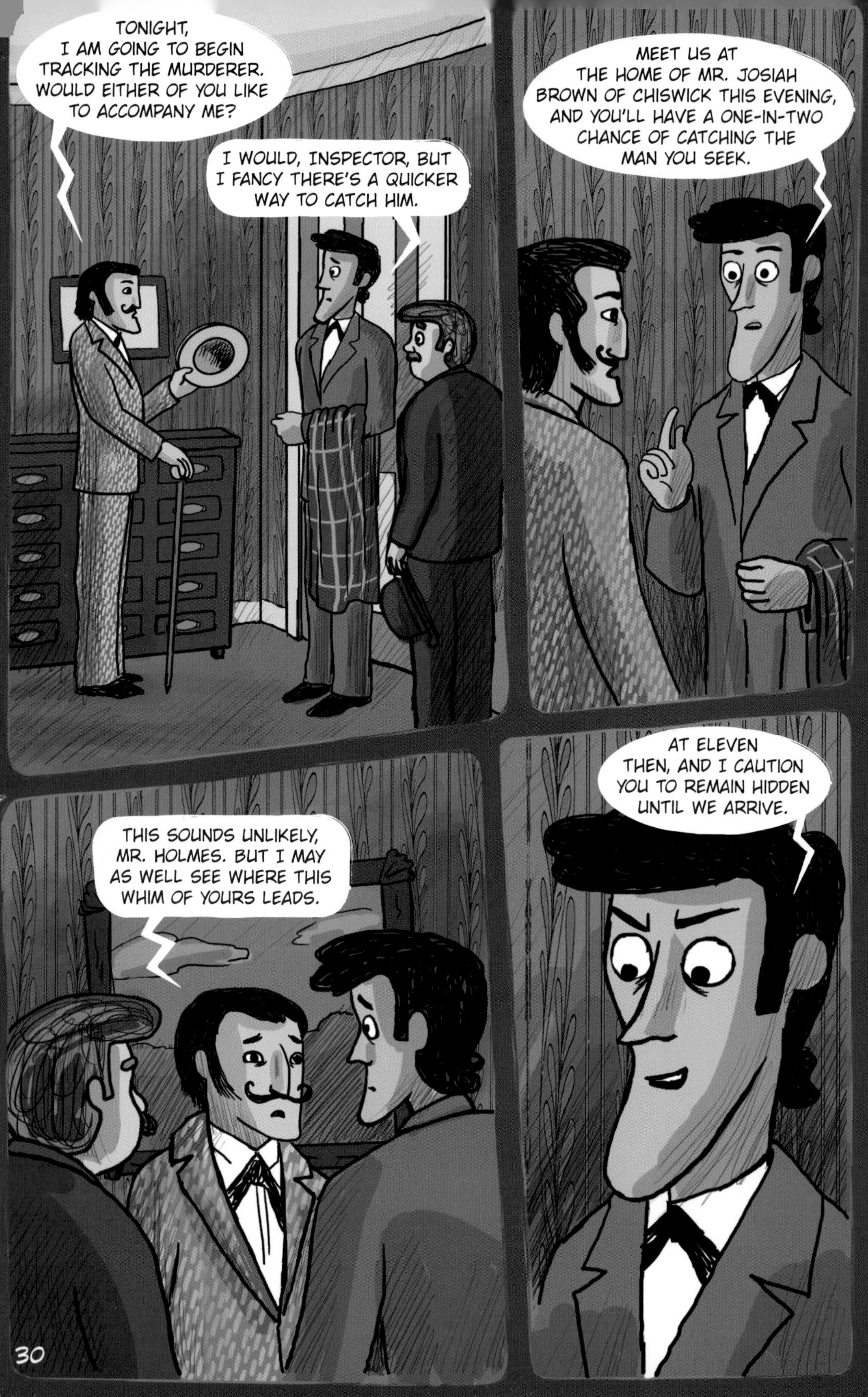
TONIGHT, I AM GOING TO BEGIN TRACKING THE MURDERER. WOULD EITHER OF YOU LIKE TO ACCOMPANY ME?
I WOULD, INSPECTOR, BUT I FANCY THERE'S A QUICKER WAY TO CATCH HIM.
MEET US AT THE HOME OF MR. JOSIAH BROWN OF CHISWICK THIS EVENING, AND YOU'LL HAVE A ONE-IN-TWO CHANCE OF CATCHING THE MAN YOU SEEK.
THIS SOUNDS UNLIKELY, MR. HOLMES. BUT I MAY AS WELL SEE WHERE THIS WHIM OF YOURS LEADS.
AT ELEVEN THEN, AND I CAUTION YOU TO REMAIN HIDDEN UNTIL WE ARRIVE.

After Lestrade left, Holmes sent a letter by express messenger to Mr. Brown of Chiswick, informing him of our evening plans. Then he sent a telegram to Mr. Sandeford of Reading, asking him to come to Baker Street the next day.

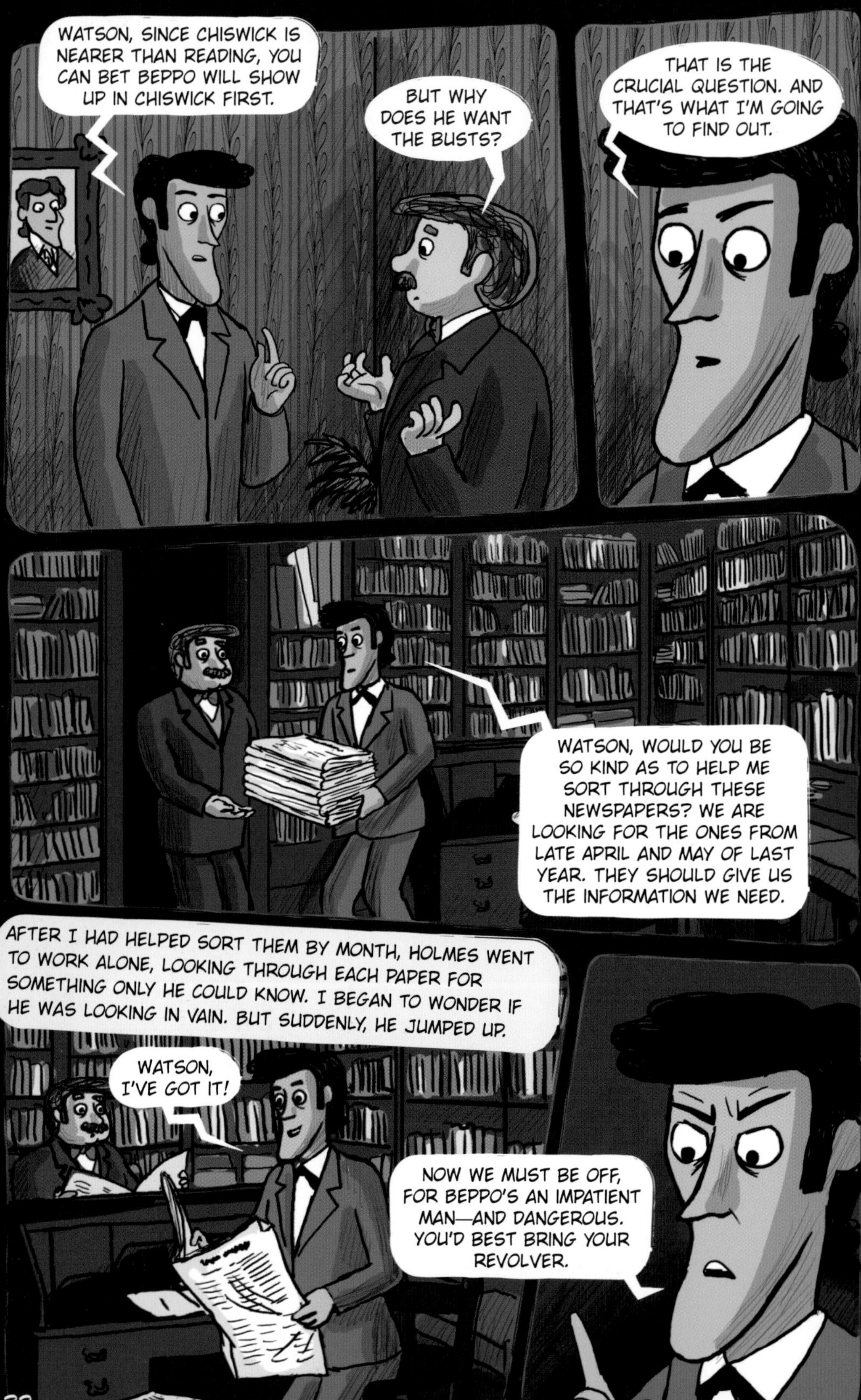

WATSON, SINCE CHISWICK IS NEARER THAN READING, YOU CAN BET BEPPO WILL SHOW UP IN CHISWICK FIRST.
BUT WHY DOES HE WANT THE BUSTS?
THAT IS THE CRUCIAL QUESTION. AND THAT'S WHAT I'M GOING TO FIND OUT.
WATSON, WOULD YOU BE SO KIND AS TO HELP ME SORT THROUGH THESE NEWSPAPERS? WE ARE LOOKING FOR THE ONES FROM LATE APRIL AND MAY OF LAST YEAR. THEY SHOULD GIVE US THE INFORMATION WE NEED.
AFTER I HAD HELPED SORT THEM BY MONTH, HOLMES WENT TO WORK ALONE, LOOKING THROUGH EACH PAPER FOR SOMETHING ONLY HE COULD KNOW. I BEGAN TO WONDER IF HE WAS LOOKING IN VAIN. BUT SUDDENLY, HE JUMPED UP.
WATSON, I'VE GOT IT!
NOW WE MUST BE OFF, FOR BEPPO'S AN IMPATIENT MAN—AND DANGEROUS. YOU'D BEST BRING YOUR REVOLVER.

June 7, 1895, 10:00 p.m.

So in due haste, Holmes and I headed for the street and hailed a cab for the long drive to Chiswick. About a block from Brown's house, Holmes had the cabby stop the carriage, and we walked the rest of the way. The darkness and fog of the night were settling in. As we neared Brown's home, Lestrade appeared from behind a hedge. Silently, the three of us crept to the side of the house.

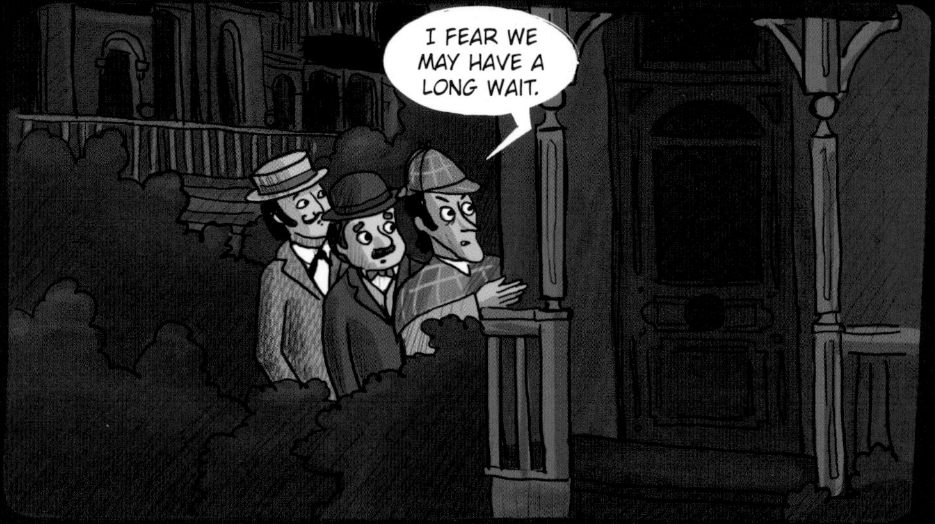
I FEAR WE MAY HAVE A LONG WAIT.

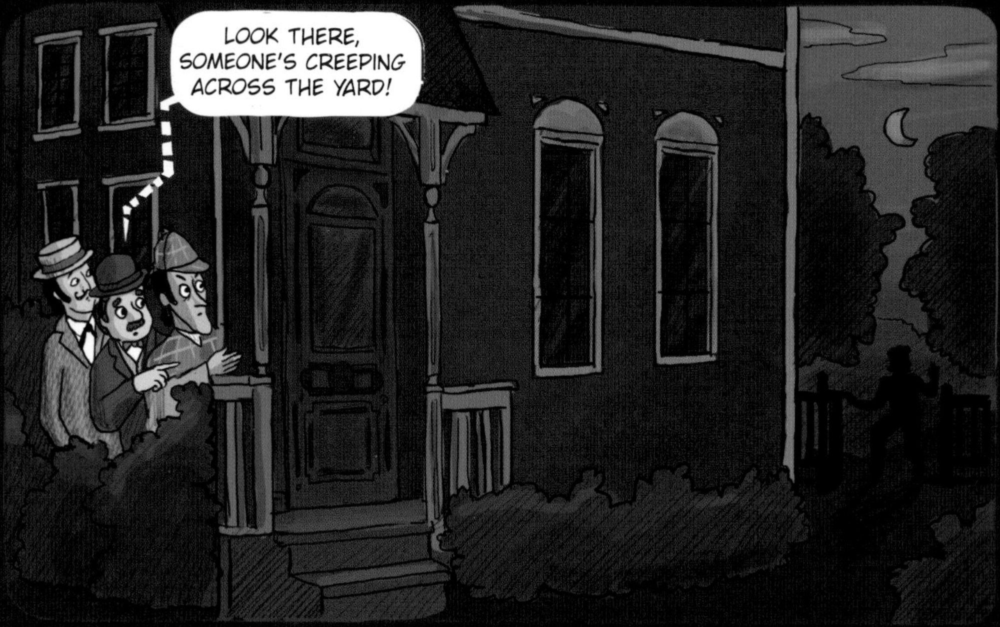
LOOK THERE, SOMEONE'S CREEPING ACROSS THE YARD!

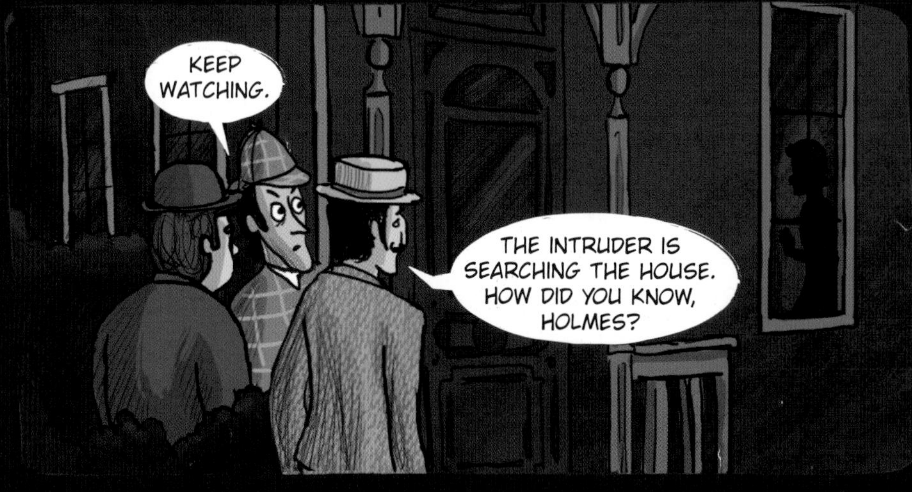
KEEP WATCHING.
THE INTRUDER IS SEARCHING THE HOUSE. HOW DID YOU KNOW, HOLMES?

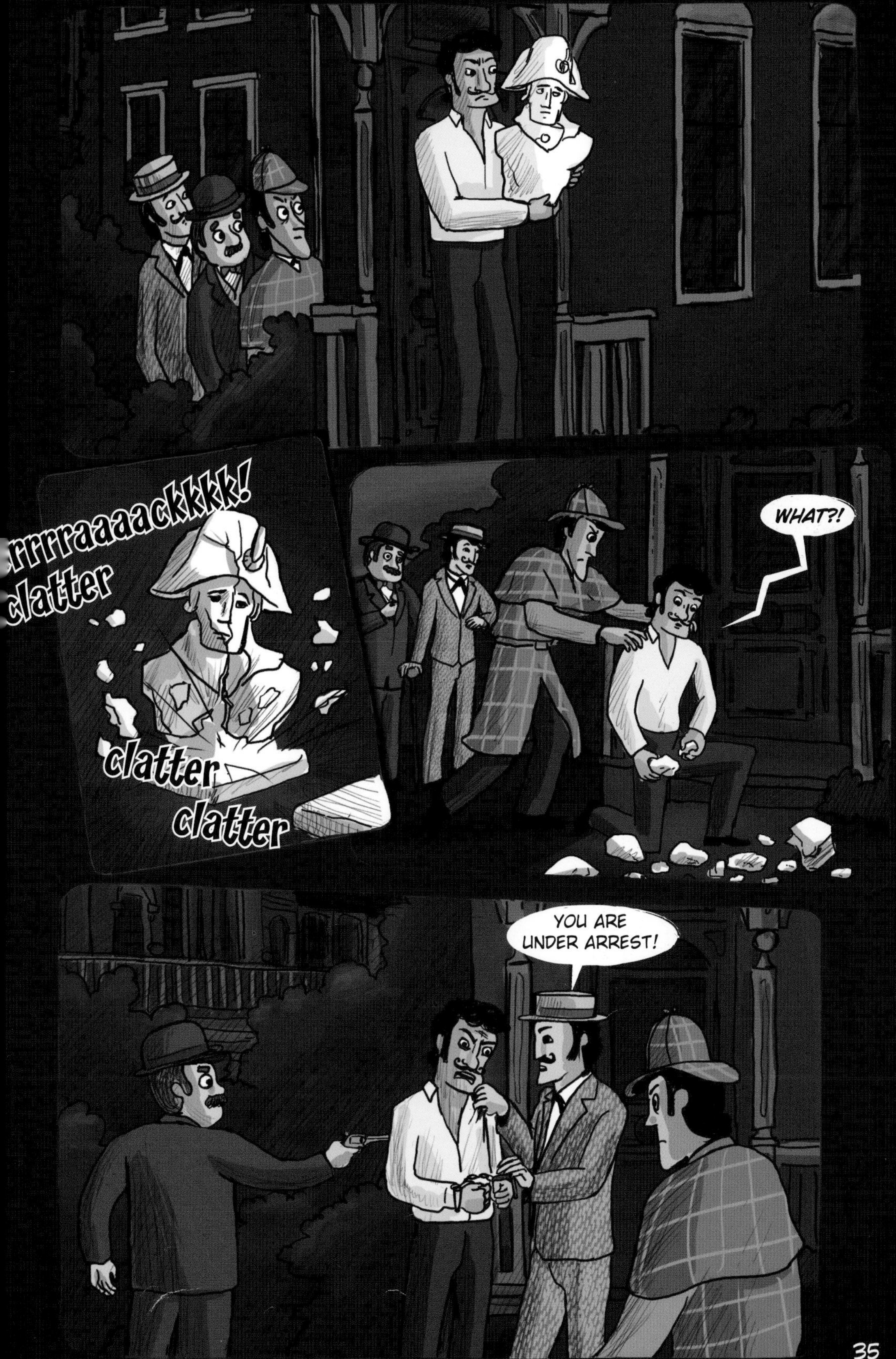
rrrraaaackkkk!
clatter
clatter
clatter
WHAT?!
YOU ARE UNDER ARREST!

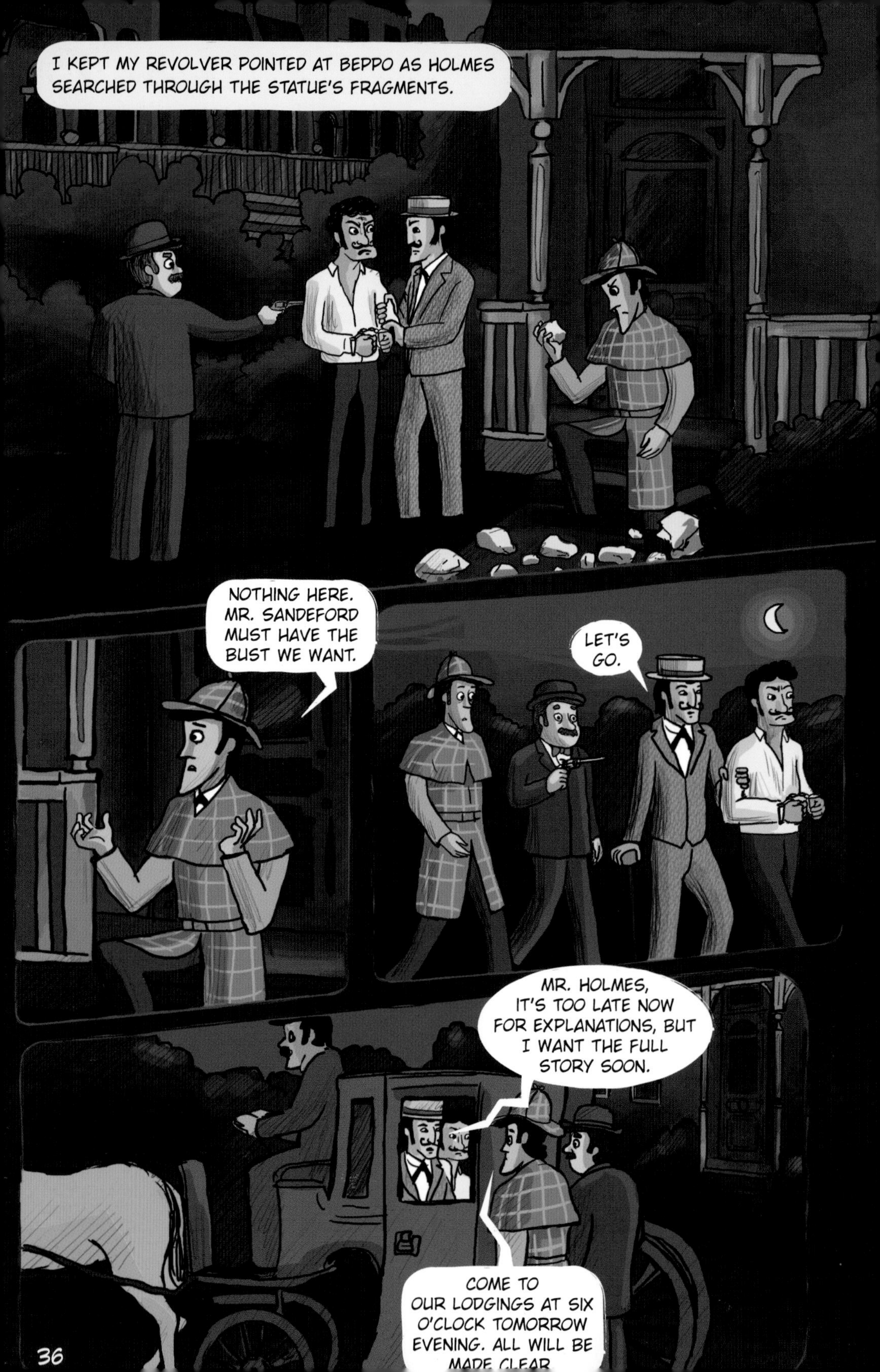
I KEPT MY REVOLVER POINTED AT BEPPO AS HOLMES SEARCHED THROUGH THE STATUE'S FRAGMENTS.
NOTHING HERE. MR. SANDEFORD MUST HAVE THE BUST WE WANT.
LET'S GO.
MR. HOLMES, IT'S TOO LATE NOW FOR EXPLANATIONS, BUT I WANT THE FULL STORY SOON.
COME TO OUR LODGINGS AT SIX O'CLOCK TOMORROW EVENING. ALL WILL BE MADE CLEAR

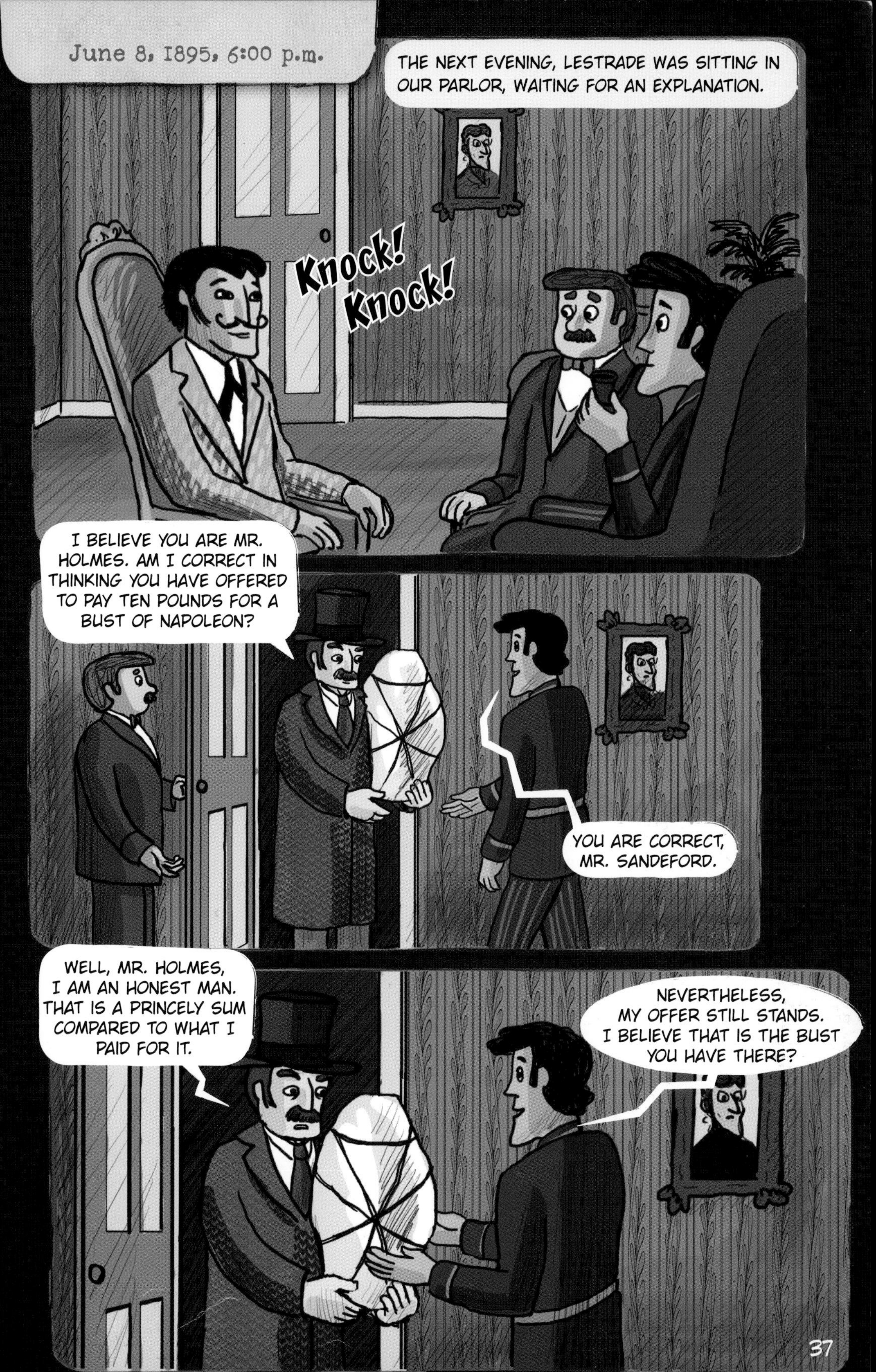
June 8, 1895, 6:00 p.m.
THE NEXT EVENING, LESTRADE WAS SITTING IN OUR PARLOR, WAITING FOR AN EXPLANATION.
Knock! Knock!
I BELIEVE YOU ARE MR. HOLMES. AM I CORRECT IN THINKING YOU HAVE OFFERED TO PAY TEN POUNDS FOR A BUST OF NAPOLEON?
YOU ARE CORRECT, MR. SANDEFORD.
WELL, MR. HOLMES, I AM AN HONEST MAN. THAT IS A PRINCELY SUM COMPARED TO WHAT I PAID FOR IT.
NEVERTHELESS, MY OFFER STILL STANDS. I BELIEVE THAT IS THE BUST YOU HAVE THERE?

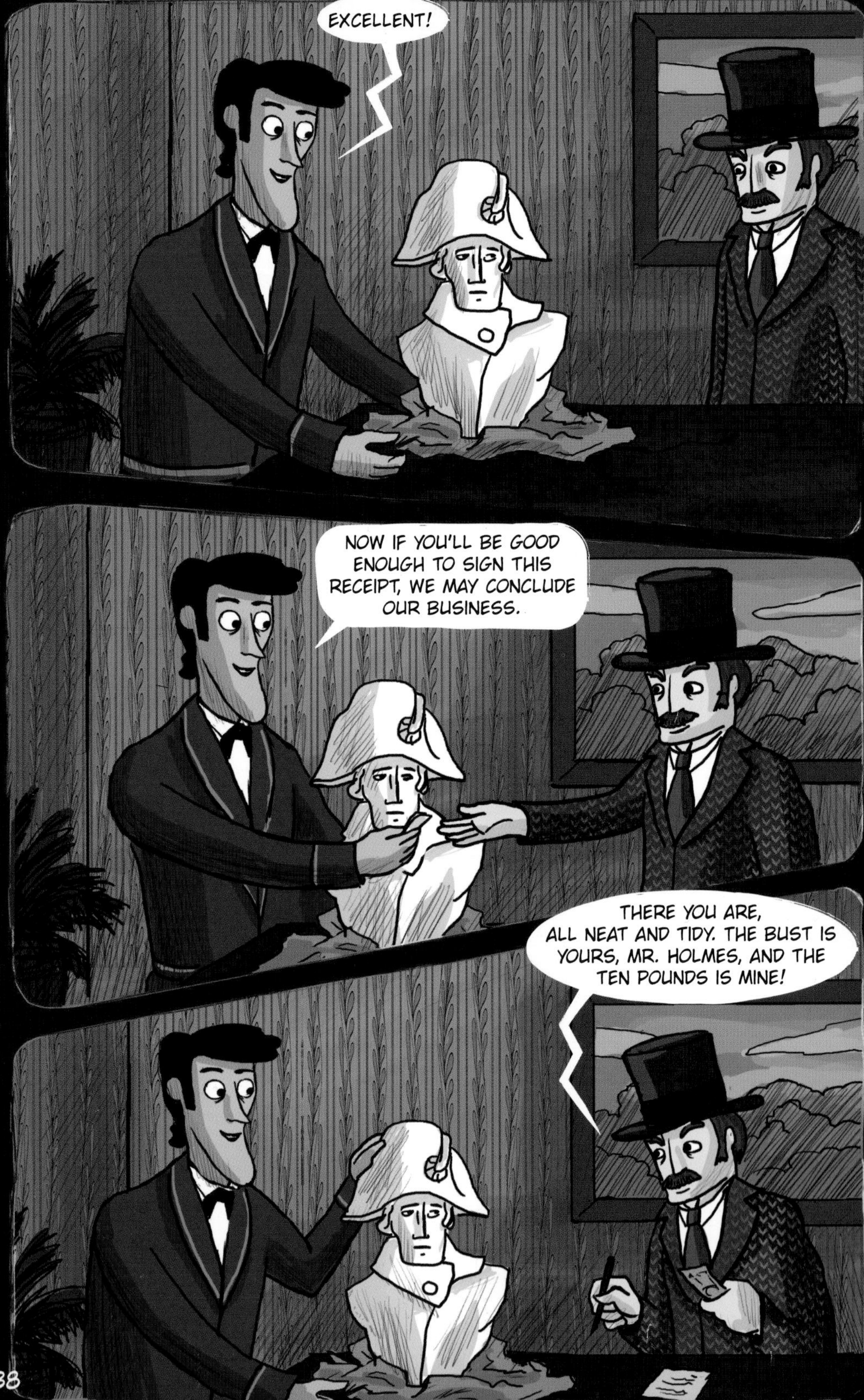
EXCELLENT!
NOW IF YOU'LL BE GOOD ENOUGH TO SIGN THIS RECEIPT, WE MAY CONCLUDE OUR BUSINESS.
THERE YOU ARE, ALL NEAT AND TIDY. THE BUST IS YOURS, MR. HOLMES, AND THE TEN POUNDS IS MINE!

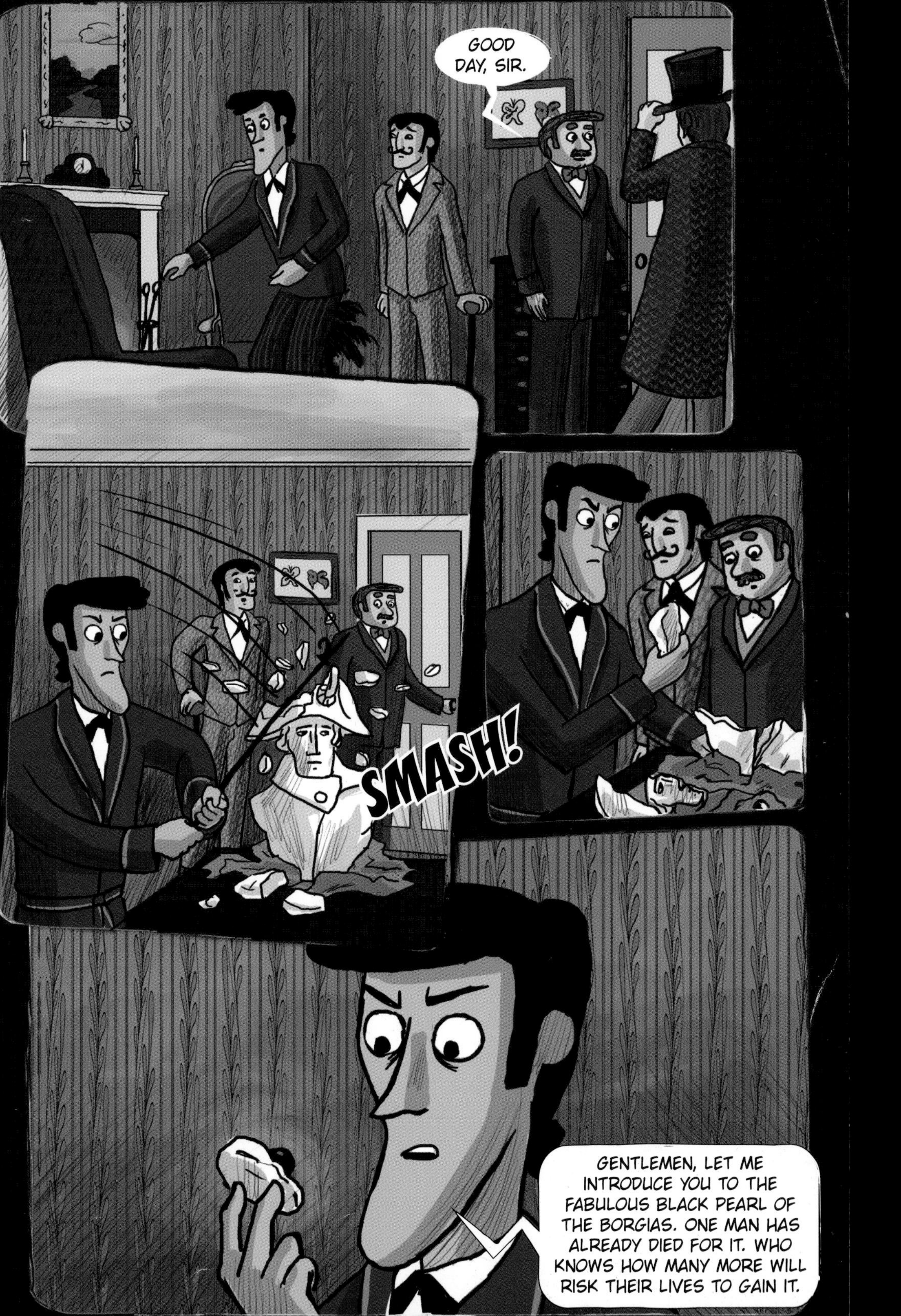

GOOD DAY, SIR.
SMASH!
GENTLEMEN, LET ME INTRODUCE YOU TO THE FABULOUS BLACK PEARL OF THE BORGIAS. ONE MAN HAS ALREADY DIED FOR IT. WHO KNOWS HOW MANY MORE WILL RISK THEIR LIVES TO GAIN IT.

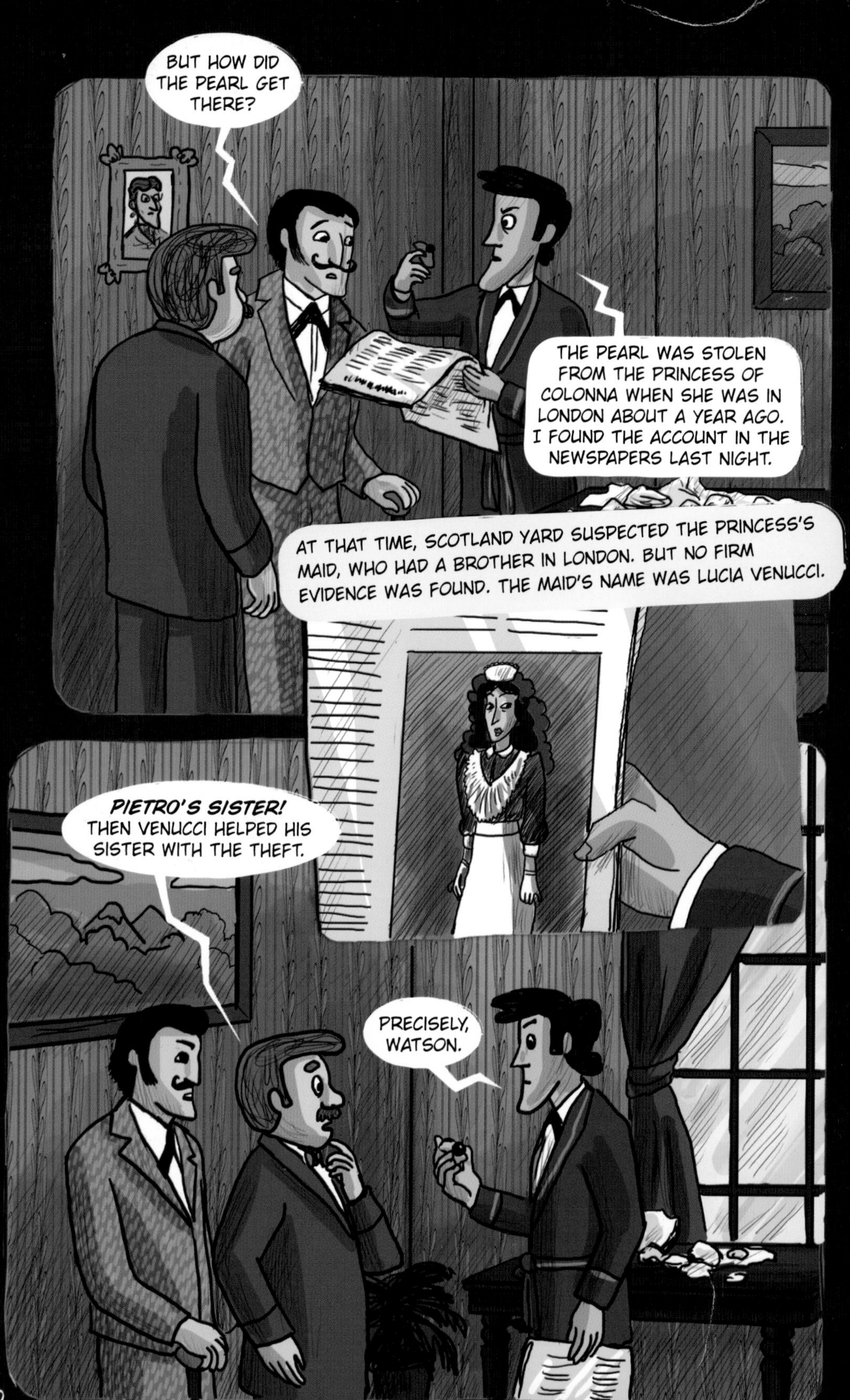

BUT HOW DID THE PEARL GET THERE?
THE PEARL WAS STOLEN FROM THE PRINCESS OF COLONNA WHEN SHE WAS IN LONDON ABOUT A YEAR AGO. I FOUND THE ACCOUNT IN THE NEWSPAPERS LAST NIGHT.
AT THAT TIME, SCOTLAND YARD SUSPECTED THE PRINCESS'S MAID, WHO HAD A BROTHER IN LONDON. BUT NO FIRM EVIDENCE WAS FOUND. THE MAID'S NAME WAS LUCIA VENUCCI.
PIETRO'S SISTER! THEN VENUCCI HELPED HIS SISTER WITH THE THEFT.
PRECISELY, WATSON.

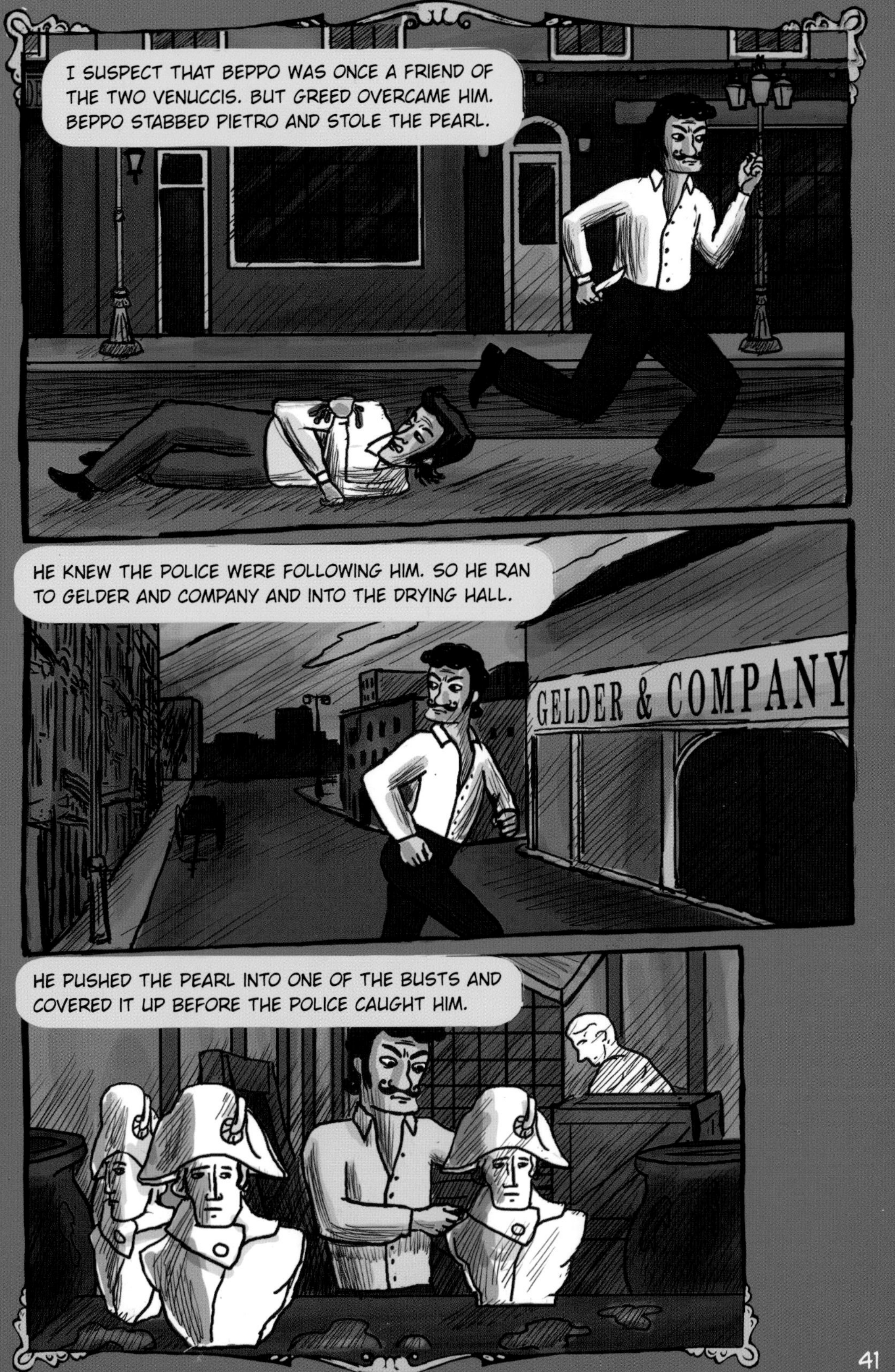
I SUSPECT THAT BEPPO WAS ONCE A FRIEND OF THE TWO VENUCCIS. BUT GREED OVERCAME HIM. BEPPO STABBED PIETRO AND STOLE THE PEARL.
HE KNEW THE POLICE WERE FOLLOWING HIM. SO HE RAN TO GELDER AND COMPANY AND INTO THE DRYING HALL.
GELDER & COMPANY
HE PUSHED THE PEARL INTO ONE OF THE BUSTS AND COVERED IT UP BEFORE THE POLICE CAUGHT HIM.

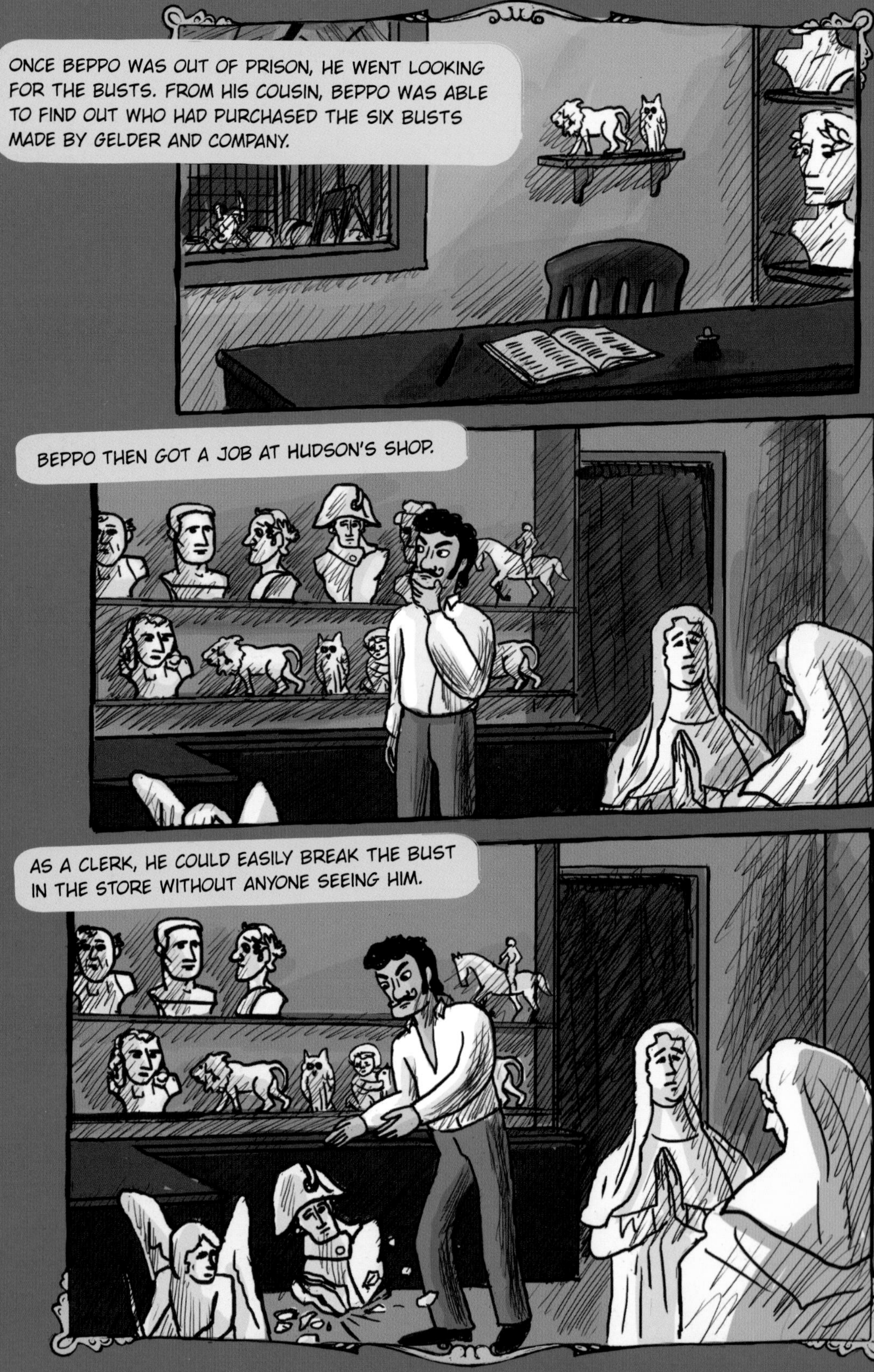
ONCE BEPPO WAS OUT OF PRISON, HE WENT LOOKING FOR THE BUSTS. FROM HIS COUSIN, BEPPO WAS ABLE TO FIND OUT WHO HAD PURCHASED THE SIX BUSTS MADE BY GELDER AND COMPANY.
BEPPO THEN GOT A JOB AT HUDSON'S SHOP.
AS A CLERK, HE COULD EASILY BREAK THE BUST IN THE STORE WITHOUT ANYONE SEEING HIM.

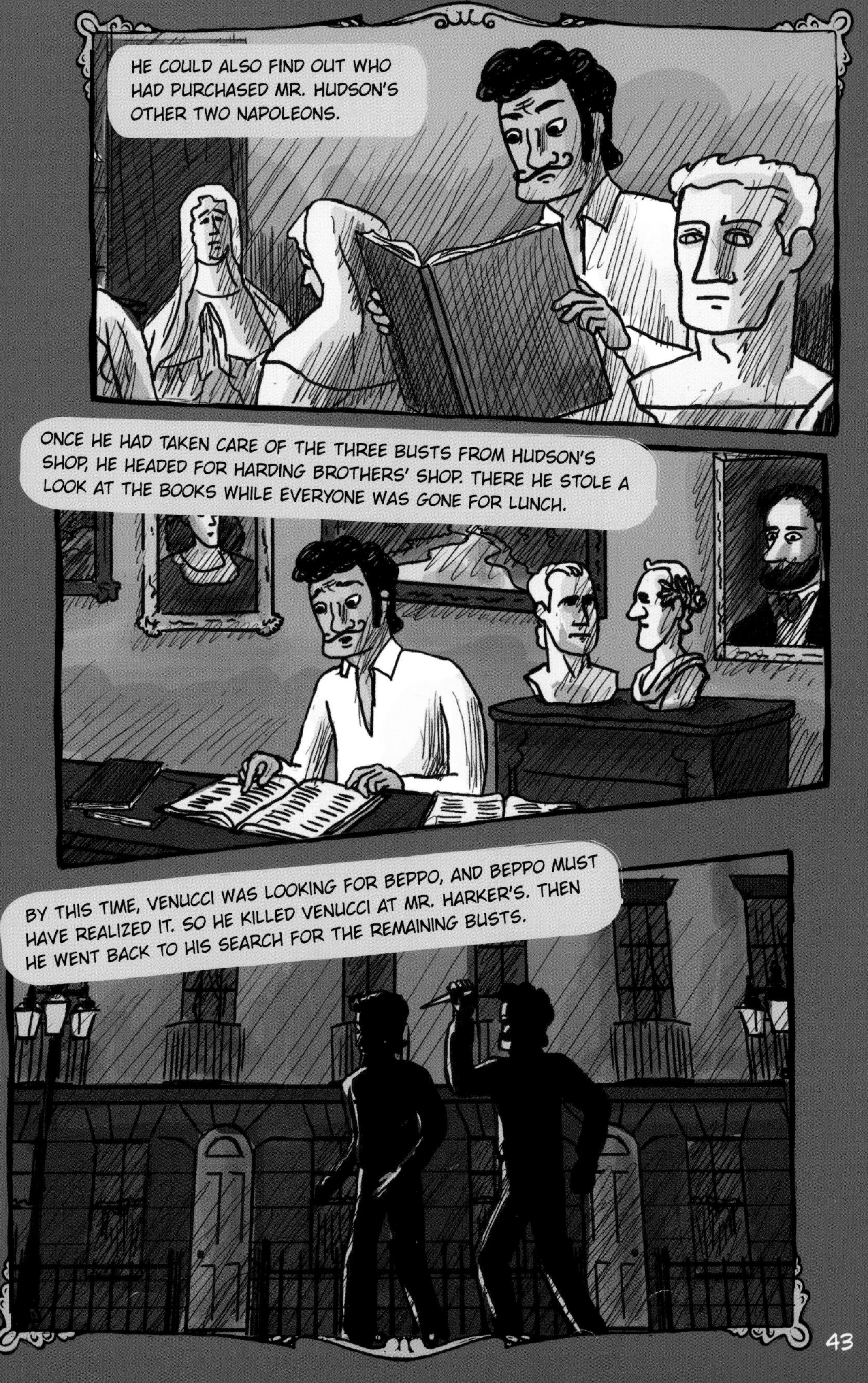
HE COULD ALSO FIND OUT WHO HAD PURCHASED MR. HUDSON'S OTHER TWO NAPOLEONS.
ONCE HE HAD TAKEN CARE OF THE THREE BUSTS FROM HUDSON'S SHOP, HE HEADED FOR HARDING BROTHERS' SHOP. THERE HE STOLE A LOOK AT THE BOOKS WHILE EVERYONE WAS GONE FOR LUNCH.
BY THIS TIME, VENUCCI WAS LOOKING FOR BEPPO, AND BEPPO MUST HAVE REALIZED IT. SO HE KILLED VENUCCI AT MR. HARKER'S. THEN HE WENT BACK TO HIS SEARCH FOR THE REMAINING BUSTS.

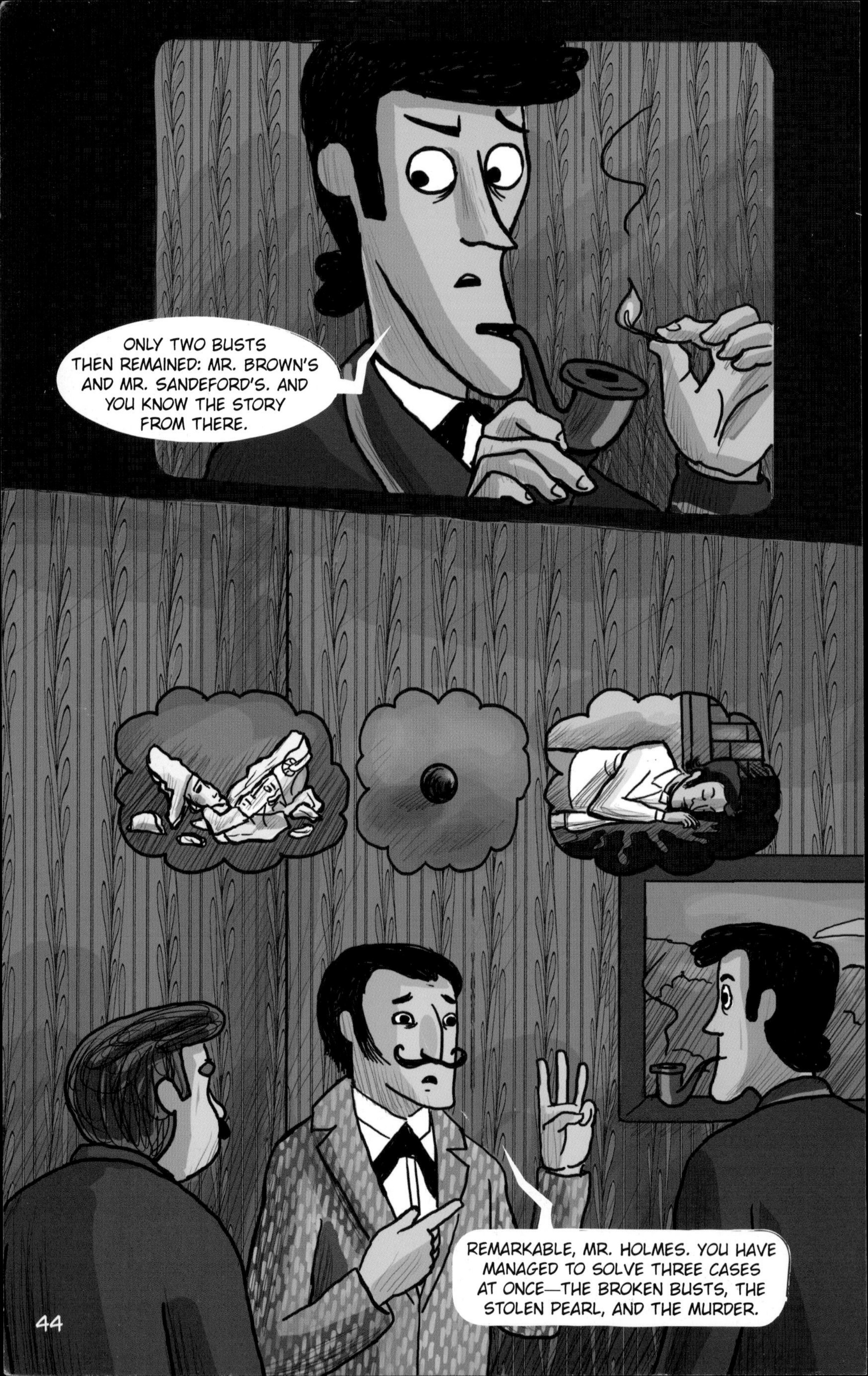
ONLY TWO BUSTS THEN REMAINED: MR. BROWN'S AND MR. SANDEFORD'S. AND YOU KNOW THE STORY FROM THERE.
REMARKABLE, MR. HOLMES. YOU HAVE MANAGED TO SOLVE THREE CASES AT ONCE—THE BROKEN BUSTS, THE STOLEN PEARL, AND THE MURDER.

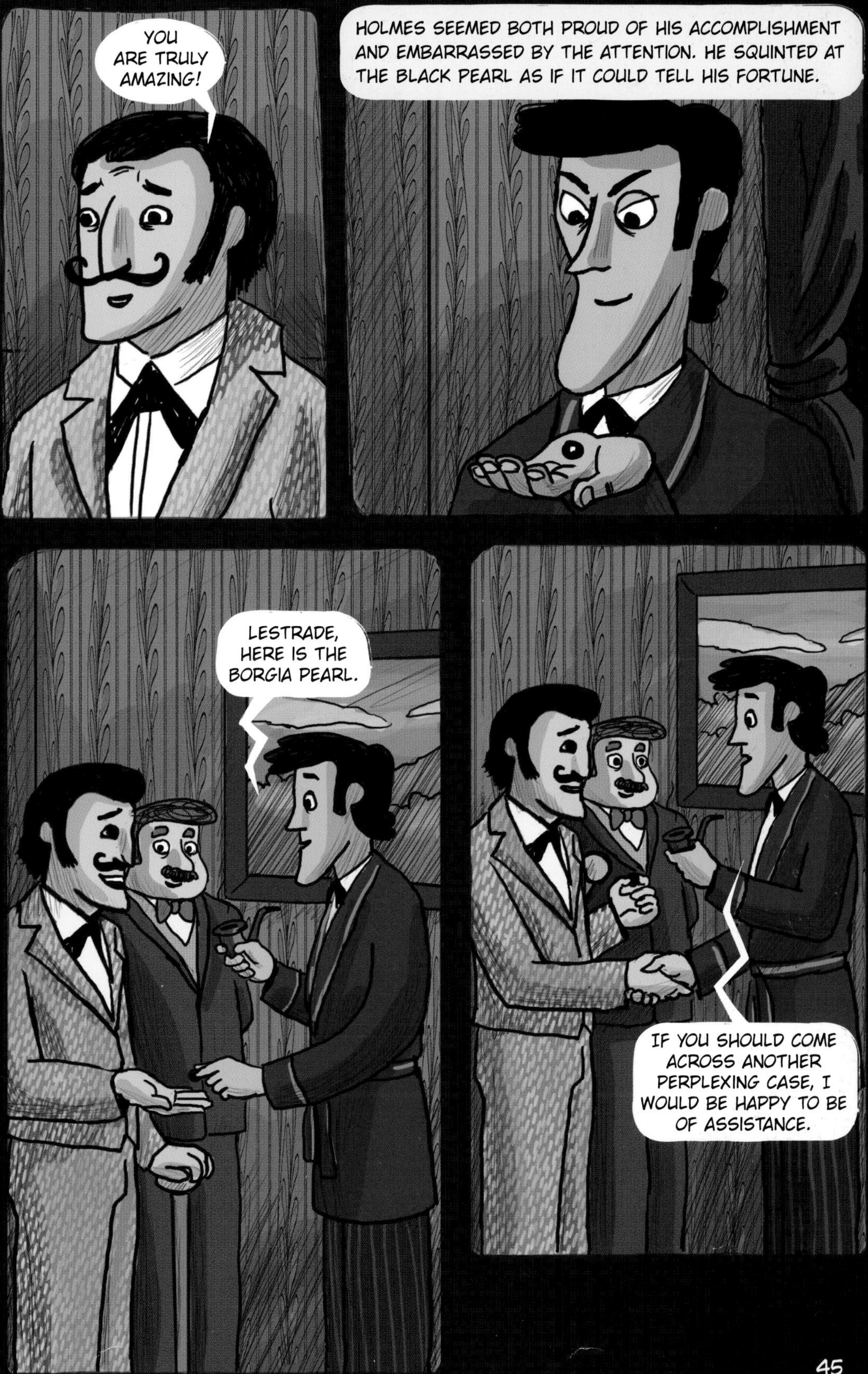
YOU ARE TRULY AMAZING!
HOLMES SEEMED BOTH PROUD OF HIS ACCOMPLISHMENT AND EMBARRASSED BY THE ATTENTION. HE SQUINTED AT THE BLACK PEARL AS IF IT COULD TELL HIS FORTUNE.
LESTRADE, HERE IS THE BORGIA PEARL.
IF YOU SHOULD COME ACROSS ANOTHER PERPLEXING CASE, I WOULD BE HAPPY TO BE OF ASSISTANCE.

From the Desk of
John H. Watson, M.D.

The Adventure of the Six Napoleons: How Did Holmes Solve It?

How was Holmes able to figure out that the bust smashing wasn't a case of hatred for Napoleon?

Lestrade believed that the bust smasher hated Napoleon. Holmes, however, suspected that it was the bust itself that was important, not Napoleon. The thief seemed to be looking for a particular bust out of a group of look-alikes. This theory was confirmed when Holmes discovered that all the broken busts had been cast from the same mold in a batch of six.

Holmes noticed that all the busts had been smashed where there was enough light to examine the pieces. This made him think that the criminal was looking for something of value hidden in one of the busts.

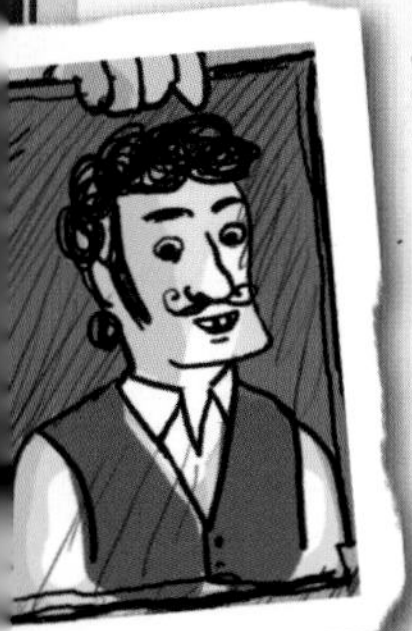

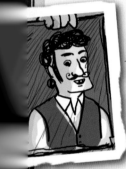

How did Holmes use the photo to help him solve the crime?

Holmes used Beppo's photo to get information. When Hudson recognized Beppo as his clerk, Holmes knew that the murder was definitely connected to the busts. Since Beppo had been a clerk in the shop at the time of the bust smashing, he was a suspect for both the murder and the thefts.

How did Holmes figure out Beppo's part in the crimes?

According to the company manager, Beppo ran to Gelder and Company after the stabbing. Why? Holmes thought it was to hide something he was carrying. Since he ran to the drying hall, Holmes figured that he could have hidden something in one of the busts that was drying. This possibility was confirmed when the manager told Holmes that the busts sold to the shops of Hudson and Harding Brothers were finished at about the same time as the arrest occurred.

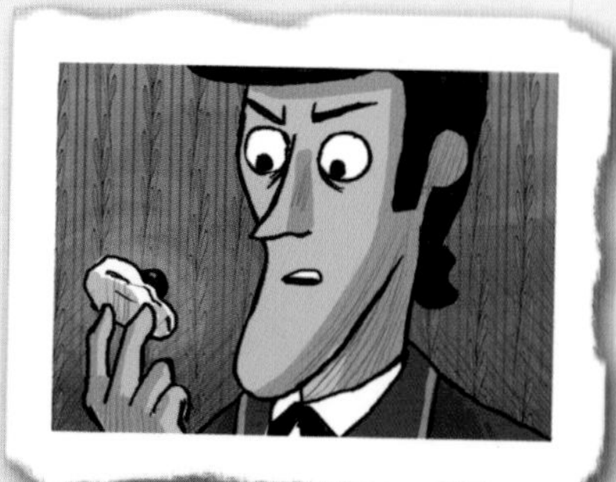

How did Holmes conclude that the stolen pearl was hidden in one of the busts?

Holmes searched the newspapers of the previous spring to find a crime that had occurred near the time that Beppo had been arrested. The theft of the Borgia pearl was exactly what he was looking for. Holmes's hunch was confirmed when he read that the maid's name was Lucia Venucci and that she had a brother in London. Holmes knew that Pietro Venucci must be the maid's brother.

Further Reading and Websites

The Beacon Society
http://beaconsociety.com/Student.html

Burleigh, Robert. *Napoleon: The Story of the Little Corporal*. New York: Abrams, 2007.

Coleman, Alice Scovall. *The Spirit of Chatsworth Mansion*. New York: Tiara Books, 2006.

Heuston, Kimberley. *Napoleon: Emperor and Conqueror*. New York: Franklin Watts, 2010.

Kassinger, Ruth. *Ceramics*. Minneapolis: Twenty-First Century Books, 2003.

O'Dell, Scott. *The Black Pearl*. New York: Sandpiper, 2010.

Sherlock Holmes Museum
http://www.sherlock-holmes.co.uk

Sir Arthur Conan Doyle Society
http://www.ash-tree.bc.ca/acdsocy.html

221 Baker Street
http://221bakerstreet.org

About the Author

Sir Arthur Conan Doyle was born on May 22, 1859. He became a doctor in 1882. When this career did not prove successful, Doyle started writing stories. In addition to the popular Sherlock Holmes short stories and novels, Doyle also wrote historical novels, romances, and plays.

About the Adapters

Murray Shaw's lifelong passion for Sherlock Holmes began when he was a child. He was the author of the Match Wits with Sherlock Holmes series published in the 1990s. For decades, he was a popular speaker in public schools and libraries on the adventures of Holmes and Watson.

M. J. Cosson is the author of more than fifty books, both fiction and nonfiction, for children and young adults. She has long been a fan of mysteries and especially of the great detective, Sherlock Holmes. In fact, she has participated in the production of several Sherlock Holmes plays. A native of Iowa, Cosson lives in the Texas Hill Country with her husband, dogs, and cat.

About the Illustrators

Sophie Rohrbach began her career after graduating in display design at the Chambre des Commerce in France. She went on to design displays in many top department stores including Galerias Lafayette. She also studied illustration at Emile Cohl school in Lyon, France, where she now lives with her daughter. Rohrbach has illustrated many children's books. She is passionate about the colors and patterns that she uses in her illustrations.

JT Morrow has worked as a freelance illustrator for over twenty years and has won several awards. He specializes in doing parodies and imitations of the Old and Modern Masters—everyone from da Vinci to Picasso. JT also exhibits his paintings at galleries near his home. He lives just south of San Francisco with his wife and daughter.